A Scandal in Belgravia

Also by Robert Barnard
in Thorndike Large Print

A City of Strangers
Death and the Chaste Apprentice
At Death's Door
The Skeleton in the Grass
The Cherry Blossom Corpse
Bodies

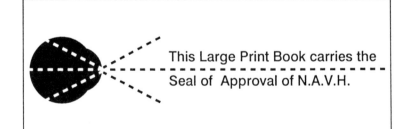

This Large Print Book carries the
Seal of Approval of N.A.V.H.

ROBERT BARNARD

A Scandal in Belgravia

THORNDIKE ~ MAGNA

Thorndike, Maine U.S.A.
North Yorkshire, England

Library of Congress Cataloging in Publication Data:
Barnard, Robert.
    A scandal in Belgravia / Robert Barnard.
        p.   cm.
    ISBN 1-56054-283-7 (alk. paper : lg. print)
    1. Large type books. I. Title.
    [PR6052.A665S33   1991b]   91-36294
    823'.914—dc20   CIP

British Library Cataloging in Publication Data:

A catalogue record for this book is available from the
British Library.
ISBN 0-75050-395-9

This is a work of fiction. Names, characters, places, and
incidents either are the product of the author's imagination
or are used fictitiously. Any resemblance to events or
persons, living or dead, is entirely coincidental.

Thorndike Press Large Print edition published in 1992
by arrangement with Charles Scribner's Sons.

Large Print edition available in the British Commonwealth by arrangement with Transworld Publishers Ltd.

Cover design by Carol Pringle.

The tree indicium is a trademark of Thorndike Press.

This book is printed on acid-free, high opacity paper.

A Scandal in Belgravia

1

EVENING in the PARK

I have never thought of myself as a writer, so I have never imagined myself suffering from writer's block. Yet that, surely, must be what is preventing me writing.

Whenever I sit down at my desk to organise my thoughts, perhaps even sketch out a page or two, the figure that strolls insistently yet engagingly into my mind is always that of Timothy Wycliffe. He pops in, just as he used to pop into my office all those years ago, banishing the earnest intentions I had of getting down to some solid work. So insistent is this memory of him — laughing, incisive, shocking, as he used to be in life — that I seem totally unable to get down to any coherent narrative of those times.

It should be an easy, straightforward chapter to write, the story of the early 1950s — a dullish period in my life. I knocked off the first chapter (birth, family, education, humdrum army experiences at the end of the war,

7

Oxford) with an ease that must have been deceptive, though I would not pretend there is any literary grace in the telling. I know that my early life was not of the stuff that the Sunday newspapers will be interested in serialising. What they will want is gossip about my fellow politicians, particularly those still in the public eye, and more especially dirt on the respected former Prime Minister who sacked me. The latter I shall dole out sparingly, if at all. It ill behoves a cabinet minister relieved of his post to bite the hand that hitherto had fed him, though most do. But certainly one period that will not interest the *Sunday Times* — inevitably it will be, I suspect, the *Sunday Times* — is my years as a fledgling diplomat at the Foreign Office. A brief, factual narrative is all that is required, and I should be able to sew it up in a dry ten pages or so. Yet it is not happening. Quite against my will Timothy is taking me over. Every time I take up my pen in he strolls, with the same sort of smile on his face as he had when he used to stroll up to my desk. And I know that the words will not come because my mind is taken over by that elegant, teasing, casually outrageous figure — my friend and colleague Timothy Wycliffe.

I do not think it is because he was murdered. That was five years later, and by that time contact between us was casual and occasional. In fact, I'm afraid that his murder made less impact on me at the time than it should have done: it was something brutal, shocking, but I quite soon put it out of my mind. And yet in those years when we were together on the lowest rungs of the Foreign Office ladder we were really very close.

If I try to analyse that closeness I can see that his background dazzled me a little. His grandfather was the Marquess of Redmond — and even I, a middle-class Londoner who had been a day-boy at Dulwich, knew that a Marquess was something. His father was Lord John Wycliffe, a younger son, and said by some to be a rising star in the Conservative Party, though there were others at that time who said that figures such as he, who had acquired a Commons seat almost by family right, were increasingly out-of-date in Tory politics. Anyway it is likely that his family background helped Timothy to get into the Foreign Office, though, equally, there was no doubt that he was bright, bright in every way — a sharp, uncluttered brain, with an imagination to match. I was dazzled by him personally quite as much as I was dazzled by his pedigree.

"We're the new boys here," he said to me when we were introduced, "so we see things more clearly than the old hands."

In fact he had been there about six weeks or so when I started, but essentially we learned the ropes and found our feet together. It was a testing time for both of us. This was early in 1951, in the dying days of the Labour government, when people were already envisioning Churchill's return as Prime Minister. It was also a time when problems, inevitable but unforeseen, were piling up. In particular my early days in the Foreign Office coincided with Burgess and Maclean absconding to the Soviet Union to avoid exposure as Russian agents, and with British oil interests in Persia (as most of us still called Iran) being threatened by Dr. Mussadegh, with his stated intention of nationalising the oil companies.

A baptism of fire indeed! In fact I don't remember discussing the former subject except very briefly and in hushed tones. I was too junior, and everyone was trying in vain to keep the matter under wraps. It was, so to speak, taken up on high, and we were expected to leave well alone. Security matters always lead politicians to reach for a thick blanket. A subject such as the Persian crisis, however, and our new Foreign Secretary's handling of it, was fair game for gossip in corridors and offices.

That is my first substantial memory of Tim — as opposed to a general sense of brightness and friendliness. We had both been working late, well into the evening one warm summer's day in June. What we were doing was certainly not important, but nevertheless it was pressing. We would be judged by the speed and competence with which we handled it. Finally, when it was put to bed, Tim landed up in my office with two cups of black coffee (nowadays I suspect it would be Scotch, for we have become a much more alcoholic nation), and we settled down for a good gossip. Inevitably the talk turned to "Herbie" — Herbert Morrison, the new Foreign Secretary, for whom the F.O. had several nicknames, not all of them affectionate.

"The trouble with Herbie," I remember complaining to Tim that night, "is that he gives the impression in the House that he's not on top of his brief. *I* don't know if he is, and I don't suppose you do either, but the impression is what counts."

"He's still feeling his way," said Tim. He jumped off my desk and did an imitation of Morrison, his cock-sparrow walk along the corridors, with his little eyes darting everywhere, as if he feared a stab in the back. "The F.O. is a daunting task to take on. Give him time and he may rise to it."

"It's time he's not likely to get," I pointed out. "Attlee's almost sure to go to the country in the autumn."

"True. Then we'll get Eden for sure. And don't be fooled by the public image of *him*."

"Not nice?"

Tim frowned.

"I think he may be a perfectly good, well-meaning man. But there's something there — some unsureness. He can get frightfully prima-donnaish, and then he's hell to work for." Tim of course had never worked for Eden. I took such knowledge to be part of his birthright, springing from the political gossip that had surrounded him all his life. "So make the most of Herbie," he concluded. "A lot of the criticism is just journalistic niggling."

"Eu*phrates*," I said, quoting Herbie's two-syllable version of it that had aroused the mirth of newspapers.

"That's right. Winston and Bevin could mangle foreign names: they'd wrestle with a really odd one, and it'd land up on the ropes, badly mauled. People thought it was endearing, a patriotic trait even. Herbie does the same thing, but he does it more tentatively, and everyone laughs themselves sick. Herbie knows they wouldn't have laughed at Bevin, and that Bevin wouldn't have worried if they did. And that makes it worse. They loathed each other."

"Then he should damned well master his text," I said.

"His mind is on other things."

"Well, it shouldn't be. What things, anyway?"

Tim nodded his head towards the South Bank, currently occupied by the Festival of Britain — the Festival Hall, the Dome of Discovery, and all those other constructions long since gone. Does anyone remember the Festival of Britain today? It was very much the creation of the Labour government, and much mocked in the newspapers, but I remember having an awful lot of fun there.

"The Festival is his baby," Tim said. "He loves it. It's what he wants to be remembered by. He's of an age when politicians start looking for monuments."

How true that was, and how we have suffered since from politicians anxious to leave monuments! It strikes me that Timothy Wycliffe's conversation was shot through with political insights which got to the heart of the matter — that illuminated things that I only now, after a quarter of a century in politics, am beginning to understand. It can't have been just his growing up in a political household, especially as I never got the impression he and his father were particularly close, or that he had sat at his feet politically. I think

13

it was his own perceptive, incisive intellect that taught him so much so early about the game of politics, and about politicians and their ways.

I have set down all I remember about that first conversation I had with him that did not concern day-to-day business. But I have one strong visual memory of him too: Timothy, sitting on my desk, slim, elegant, intensely alive, with the long lock of fair hair falling over his eyes to give a misleading impression of dandyism, of the dated aesthete.

Alive — that is, sadly, the word that sums him up for me. Alive, joyful, thirsty for experience, with a relish for all kinds of people and an ever-present sense of the ridiculous.

Quite by chance we finished the other pieces of low-level drudgery we were engaged on at the same time, so that we happened to meet at the King Charles Street door. We walked together down the steps and over to St. James's Park, talking and laughing. We were so late it was already twilight, and the park — much my favourite of all the London parks — was looking magical. We were still laughing, I remember, when we separated at the point where our paths diverged, Tim to go towards the Palace and then on to Belgravia where he lived, I to go to the St. James's Park tube station.

I dallied a little. I was still living with my parents in Dulwich at that time, and there was no reason for me to hurry home. The air was fresh and bracing, and I was still a little intoxicated at being a part — an oh-so-tiny part — of great international events. An off-duty guardsman crossed the path in front of me and a courting couple hugging each other close. I remember loitering along, and I remember before I left the park turning towards the Palace, perhaps with some sentimental thoughts about the King, who was looking old and tired, and about the young Princess who would one day succeed him.

I could see a point, some way away, where two of the paths converged. I saw the off-duty guardsman I had already noticed approach it from one direction. I saw Tim Wycliffe approach it from another. I saw them both slacken pace. I saw them make some kind of contact, of eye, of word. I stood there frozen, gazing towards them, my heart beating very fast. They talked, and then I saw them walk on slowly together. Then, as the light seemed altogether to fail, I saw them go off together into the bushes.

2

BELGRAVIA

It would be impossible today to convey to anyone under the age of forty the stunned sense of shock I felt. Difficult, too, to explain my ignorance and naiveté on the subject of homosexuality. I had been to a public school, after all. I can only say that, whatever I might have learnt had I gone to Eton, I had no such experiences at Dulwich College to contribute to my sexual enlightenment. Perhaps this was due to the fact that we had so many day boys, and we tended to stick together. I was neither attractive nor charming, being known as "Plod" Proctor. So *that* subject I learnt about through the odd smutty joke, and through playground allusions of it — that is to say, I remained profoundly ignorant of it.

The fact that I was shocked I would account for by citing factors both personal and public: I was the child of conventional, middle-class parents, people doing dull jobs, leading dull lives and having dull opinions, whose automatic reaction should the topic come up in the Sunday papers was to purse their lips and shake their heads. The papers then treated court cases involving homosexual conduct in the lip-licking style they today use in reporting child sex-abuse cases, or MPs who go in for spanking sessions.

And then there was the Guy Burgess factor. Burgess had disappeared to Moscow only months before, leaving behind a legion of tales about his brazenly open homosexuality, his liaisons, his gay parties (I suppose the newspapers would have used words like "queer" and "pervert" at the time). The rumour — or was it a joke? — around the Foreign Office was that he had left as his forwarding address: "Stage door, Bolshoi Ballet." At that very time newspapers were indulging in speculation that was frankly no wilder than some of Burgess's conduct. Questions about him and his activities were being tabled daily in the House of Commons, and Herbie Morrison was struggling to answer them, or not to answer them, as is the habit of ministers when security matters come up.

That, in short, was why I was stunned by Timothy Wycliffe's going off into the bushes with a guardsman. I must have stood there for all of a minute before I resumed my walk to the Underground. If I was unduly thoughtful when I got home it was so close to bedtime that my parents did not notice. No doubt my mother made me a mug of Horlicks and we all turned in to sleep the sleep of the just. I lived, as I say, in a very dull household, and it was all light years away from grandsons of Marquesses and encounters with guardsmen in St. James's Park.

I tried very hard next day to be the same as usual to Timothy Wycliffe. Probably I tried too hard. I am not a good actor, and this often harmed my political career. People knew what I really thought. At any rate I became convinced over the next few weeks that Timothy knew that I knew, had worked out how I knew, and was amused that I was shocked. Sometimes when he was talking to me he looked into my face and there was a satirical turning-up of the corners of his mouth that was not malicious, but seemed to express a sort of delight in the absurdity of people — in this case me. It did not affect his friendliness and openness to me, only my friendliness and openness to him.

It was perhaps two or three weeks later that our friendship reached a decisive phase — a phase when I had to make a conscious decision whether to accept or reject him and his life. How far he deliberately brought this about I never quite knew, but he did admit that he wanted it brought out into the open.

There were many quaint survivals and oddities in Foreign Office practice at that time that had not been swept away by the advent of a Labour government. Bevin was interested in policy, and the implementation of policy, and if he knew of these oddities he probably regarded them with the Olympian amusement of a Trade Union baron at the eccentricities of the upper classes. One of these survivals was that certain great folk were to be dealt with whenever possible in person, rather than by telephone or letter. However low-level the personal contact (and they didn't come lower-level than me at that time) that was how the business was to be done. The list of these great folk, some or most of them obscure and quite unknown to the general public, had apparently come about in an arbitrary way, with a rhyme and reason that was scarcely discernible to the normal human brain, and this was the only reason I can give for the fact that on an evening in July 1951 I was given the assignment of calling on Lady Thorrington in Belgrave Square.

"A question of residency rights for three displaced persons," I grumbled to Timothy in the course of the day. "And for that I have to traipse all the way over to Belgrave Square to deliver the papers in person."

"My neck of the woods," said Tim. "I'll

19

collect you later and we'll go together."

He turned up in my tiny office around four thirty, much earlier than need be, saying it was a fine afternoon and we deserved a break. Again we left the rambling pile of the Foreign Office, walked down the steps from King Charles Street, and began across the park. At least I'm keeping him from accosting guardsmen, I thought — a mean little thought, probably springing from embarrassment. We kept up a vigorous conversation, perhaps on my part to prevent him bringing up the question of my knowledge. We discussed, I remember, the Belgian king's abdication, and the prospects for the new king. I forecast that the country would be a republic within a year (my opinions on foreign affairs at that time were almost invariably wrong, which is still the case with many officials in the Foreign Office today). Tim put forward the idea that monarchies had usually survived in the twentieth century in countries with strong Labour Parties. Typically I regarded this as a brilliant paradox, though in fact it was simply a matter of intelligent observation. We had this conversation as we skirted Buckingham Palace, where the Queen's Gallery now is, and we walked on through an overcast afternoon towards Belgravia.

We were close to Belgrave Square itself

when Tim slowed down and touched me on the shoulder.

"Your appointment's for six, isn't it?" he said. "Much too early yet. Come and see my flat."

We turned into a dim little cul-de-sac called Craven Court Mews, and the apprehension that I certainly felt warred in me with a delicious sense of mixing on friendly terms well above my station. I suppose this sounds incredibly dated, even comic, to a young reader today. But the Conservative Party was not then what it is today: the party of brash new money-makers. The typical young Conservative (of whom I was one) was a snob with a social conscience. I was deliciously thrilled.

We strolled down the mews, which was paved with cobblestones and decidedly shabby, with walls that needed repainting and windows needing repointing. We were still in the era of shortages, remember, and the era when the well-heeled preferred not to show it. Timothy put his key in a door and led the way up some narrow, stuffy stairs. We passed immediately through the tiniest of hallways into a room wonderfully light, the walls washed pale blue, the furniture slim, modern, elegant — a table of rosewood and glass, chairs that looked as if they would wrap themselves round you when you sat down, and a few traditional pieces: an elegant escritoire against the wall, a long Regency dining table, a couple of family pictures. My memory — it is one of those scenes from that time that remain imprinted on my mind, and will be until I die — is of lightness, airiness, and of a brilliance that somehow laughed at the suburban clutter and knobbiness of the rooms in the detached Dulwich residence in which I had grown up. This was the perfect setting for Tim.

I became conscious, as my mind photographed this room, of the noise of water.

"Oh Lord, Heinz is still here," said Tim. He raised his voice. "Heinz — the boat train goes in an hour!" He turned to me with an open smile. "Coffee?"

I nodded nervously, suddenly wishing I hadn't come. As he moved towards the little kitchen that I could see through the door at the far end of the living room the shower was turned off in the bathroom. Seconds later a boy appeared. He was perhaps nineteen or twenty, very fair, and sturdily built. Apart from a towel over his shoulder he was quite naked.

"Sorry!" he said when he saw me, and disappeared through another door.

I sat down on one of those spare, shapely chairs, and wondered if there were two bedrooms, and if Heinz was sleeping in the main one. I immediately cursed my naiveté. Of course he was sleeping in the main one. If Timothy was a man who went with guardsmen into the bushes in the park he would not invite handsome foreign boys to his flat and then sleep in chaste isolation.

"Heinz is a friend of mine," said Timothy, appearing at the door into the kitchen.

"Oh yes?" I muttered miserably. "Is he German?"

"That's right. He's from Dresden."

I nodded, as neutrally as possible. Then suddenly I was struck by a terrible thought, and I jumped up and faced him.

"*Dresden?* But that's in —"

"East Germany? Do you know, I believe you're right."

And grinning broadly he turned back into the kitchen.

Weakly I sat down again, denied a confrontation. I felt stunned and angry. For God's sake, *East* Germany! And here I was, brought into a ménage with an aristocratic Foreign Office diplomat and a young East German homosexual. I remember actually blushing at my predicament. All my middle-class and conservative instincts rose in horror. If he didn't think about his own career, then he might have thought of mine. I blamed him bitterly, forgetting the warm glow I had felt at mingling in circles far above my own.

The bedroom door opened again. Heinz was clothed now, in flannels and a red check shirt, with a khaki knapsack on his back. He looked now like a very ordinary, nice young man. He called out "I go," and Timothy hurried from the kitchen to see him off. There was a large mirror on the wall in front of me, and I saw the two of them, in the hallway, put their arms around each other and kiss passionately on the lips.

The phrase old ladies use, "I didn't know where to put my face," is really a very apt cliché, and vividly conveys how I felt. I wanted my whole body to disappear, to crumple itself up into a little ball and hide itself away under the sofa, but above all I wanted my face to be put somewhere out of sight, where its flushed, miserable embarrassment would not give away my feelings.

The door shut, and Tim moved insouciantly back to the kitchen.

"Do you like the flat?" he asked, with a voice full of ironic amusement, as he came back with the coffee.

"Very much," I stammered, as normally as possible. "It's very . . . unusual. Stylish. It's . . . it's not the sort of furniture you see around these days."

Tim nodded, still with a smile on his lips.

"I got most of it from an aunt," he said, sitting down and pouring two cups of coffee. "She bought it in the twenties and thirties — you know, Bauhaus stuff, and imitations of it. She was something of a high-flyer, member of a rather fast set. Then a boyfriend was killed right at the start of the war, and suddenly she got religion. Sort of Anglican-cum-theosophy. For some reason she didn't think the furniture suitable any longer. She got herself a lot of heavy oak stuff, with thick tablecloths more like altar cloths — very good for séances, I suppose."

"How odd," I contributed in an unnatural voice.

"The eccentricities of our noble families! But I shouldn't mock her — she was very good to me. She died last year in the smog epidemic, and I came in for this flat as well."

He was walking round the room now, coffee cup in hand. I sat there, oddly close to tears, working up to something.

"It's a lovely room," I muttered.

"Yes. But it's an interesting story, isn't it? It shows how people regard their furniture: as a sort of stage set, to show off their view of themselves."

"So what does that make you?" I asked, marching through the conversational door he had opened.

"Frank?" Tim hazarded. "Open? Free as air."

"You staged all that, didn't you?" I blurted out suddenly.

"Staged?" He stopped beside me and stood smiling down, but not ironically now.

"You staged that scene with Heinz. To bring it all out into the open."

Tim sat down and sipped his coffee.

"I thought Heinz would be gone, as a matter of fact. He's a dear boy, but he has no sense of time. When he wasn't I . . . I took advantage of the fact. I had been wondering whether to say something over the last week or two. As it was I just behaved as I would have if you'd not been here."

I looked down into my coffee cup, feeling desperately gauche, as indeed I was.

"Why did you want to bring it out into the open?"

"Why not? You're the closest thing I have to a friend at the F.O. I don't like having secrets from my friends."

"Wouldn't it be better —"

"To keep it firmly under wraps? I don't think so."

I was angrily conscious that I was being given a secret, and a role, that I had not asked for and was most unwilling to accept. At last I spoke out, looking him full in the face.

"For God's sake don't pretend you haven't heard all the things people are saying about Guy Burgess. Or read what the newspapers are saying."

"Well?"

"This . . . sort of thing makes you a security risk."

"Peter, I am not Guy Burgess. I'm Timothy Wycliffe. You don't believe all negroes are the same, do you? Or Jews? Why should you believe all homosexuals are?"

"But it leaves you wide open to blackmail!"

"Come off it: blackmail is a danger if you're a *secret* homosexual. And that's what you're trying to persuade me to be. And, by the by, there never was a less secret homosexual than Guy. I'd heard about him and his antics long before I joined the Foreign Office. Burgess spied for Russia because he was — still is, presumably — a communist, not because he was blackmailed into it."

"But your father's a public figure. You know what the papers would do if they got hold of it."

He shrugged.

"That's something he'd have to handle. He's a politician: he can take care of himself. As to me, I'd resign from the Foreign Office. So what? No great tragedy. I'm not sure I see my role in life as a top civil servant —

or an ambassador, come to that. I came into the F.O. because I like 'Abroad' and haven't seen nearly enough of it. I can think of lots of other careers I'd just as soon take up — and probably will."

I shook my head.

"You're underestimating the harm it would do your father's career. But it's the security aspect that worries me most."

Tim leaned forward in his chair, smiling persuasively.

"Look, Peter: try to stop thinking of homosexuals as a group, eh? Like we were a Trade Union with a bloc vote at the Labour Party Conference. Because one homosexual was a bad security risk, it doesn't mean that we all are. We're individuals, left wing and right wing, happy and miserable, open and secret, rich and poor. Lump us all together and you prove you've got a *News of the World* sort of mind, and I don't believe you have. Think about it, eh, Peter?"

I nodded. I still felt miserable and uncertain, but I felt still more strongly that Timothy was someone whom I liked and would value as a friend.

"But you will be careful, won't you?" I insisted. "I mean, if Heinz had had access to Foreign Office papers —"

"I don't bring papers home. And if I

did they'd be about matters so trivial no Russian agent would give three kopeks for them. Because that's all you and I get to deal with, isn't it? You know what — you're a worrier, Peter."

He was right there too. That, until my recent forced retirement, was exactly what I was. I looked at my watch.

"I must go to Lady Thorrington's."

"That's right. Never keep a Lady waiting. Be nice to her, Peter. She's a dear old thing."

That was my first intimation that if you lived in Belgravia, even in a mews flat in Belgravia, you tended to know the other people living in Belgravia. It was at that time a sort of way-up-market village, with every other cottager a lord or lady. It also had a village system of communication and, as often as not, village standards of judgement.

I walked into the rarefied atmosphere of the Square, pondering this and much else. I found the seedy dignity of the place fascinating: I couldn't see how such an area could give off so strong a smell of money and privilege, yet undoubtedly it did. But as I took in the place and its feel I was also meditating on the scene I had just taken part in. I think that by the time I had walked around the Square and found Lady Thorrington at number forty-nine I had already decided that in the matter of

Timothy Wycliffe I was not neutral. In my still-schoolboyish but honorable way I had declared myself to be on his side.

"How's the great work going, Dad?" Jeremy asked when I came down to sherry this evening.

"Badly," I said. I explained that I had got some kind of writer's block: that I was caught up in the early fifties, distracted by my memories of a man of no historical importance who had had little influence on my life. I told him about Tim, and described what happened that first time I went to his flat. As I should have expected, he was totally mystified.

"But what was the big deal? He was a homosexual. So what?"

"You young people have no historical sense," I grumbled. "Homosexual practices were illegal then."

"So was parking on a double yellow line, I expect," said Jeremy. "Just explain to me why you were so miserable, so embarrassed. For God's sake, you must have been in your twenties by then. Long out of the nursery."

"You don't understand," I insisted. "It was a completely different climate then — climate of opinion, I mean. If you were caught you were put on trial, sent to jail."

"*That* wasn't very sensible."

"No, of course it wasn't. Everybody knew it was like locking Billy Bunter up in the tuck shop, but nevertheless that's what they went on doing. And if you didn't go to jail, there were the newspapers. You could be hounded out of practically any career. It was a different world."

"A very nasty one."

And of course he's right. Perhaps the reason that memories of Timothy Wycliffe have distracted me is that he sums up the transition from the world I grew up in to the world we live in now. A symbol, a symptom, a fingerpost. I have a feeling that I'm not going to be able to get away from him now.

3

A GROUP of NOBLE DAMES

The maid who came to the door of number forty-nine, Belgrave Square, was not dressed in the traditional manner, in black, with a neat white cap. Probably very few maids in 1951 were, except those in upper-class comedies, but somehow I'd imagined that Belgrave Square might still cling to the old uniform. She was dressed neatly but drably, in clothes that had seen a better peacetime, and she said "Mr. Proctor?" in an international interrogative that failed to hide her Central European accent. She looked anxiously at the envelope I was carrying, leaving me in no doubt that the papers I carried were for her.

"Lady Thorrington is expecting you."

When she shut the door there was a rich, pregnant hush in the house. She led the way upstairs. Lady Thorrington's sitting room was on the first floor. It was furnished in so exactly the way I had expected a sitting room in Belgravia to be furnished — shabby carpets, good pieces of furniture, dull pictures — that it was the woman I noticed, or rather the women, for she had a friend with her.

Lady Thorrington was a fleshy woman, but it was friendly fat, not at all intimidating, and her open, welcoming manner did not conceal the fact that hers was a capable, direct personality, and that she usually got what she wanted. In her common sense was allied with persistence and single-mindedness. By contrast I thought her clothes unsuitably frilly — not in the eternal schoolgirl manner of Bubbles Rothermere, just a little too partyish. I realized later that they were old clothes, let out most capably. Like her maid she was wearing clothes from the prewar era. I suspect now that many of her own clothing coupons went to the Europeans she gave her time to protecting. I remember when she died, when I was a junior minister in the Heath government, how surprised I was at the length of her *Times* obituary, and the warmth and sorrow of the addenda to it sent in by correspondents, many of them with foreign names.

"This is Lady Charlotte Wray."

Lady Charlotte was much more everyone's idea of a *grande* Belgravia *dame*. Spare, dressed entirely in black, and dogmatic in her speech, she was not a person one would lightly consider disputing with. Whether she was as wise or perceptive as she was dogmatic I was not sure. But she was to the life what we now think of as the Wendy Hiller part.

"Business first," said Lady Thorrington, making me wonder nervously what was to come second. She gestured me to a seat and sat down herself with a businesslike air. I took from the envelope the papers which notified the granting of residence rights to Käthe Möller and to her son and daughter-in-law Klaus and Hildegard. I explained the exceptional circumstances which had persuaded the Foreign Office and the Home Office to grant these rights. I saw Lady Thorrington nodding in a way that suggested not that she was acknowledging them to be exceptional, but that she was storing them up as loopholes for future use, for she maintained with various government departments a continuous yet courteous warfare on behalf of people they would much have preferred to keep out of the country. Finally I explained that the three would be eligible for naturalisation in five years time. Lady Thorrington leaned back in her chair.

"Most satisfactory," she said.

"*Most,*" agreed Lady Charlotte. "I shall have great pleasure in giving the news to Klaus and Hildegard."

Lady Thorrington smiled and went to the door. I had guessed that Käthe was the woman who had let me in, and she was waiting if not listening outside. I heard uninhibited expressions of joy, and heard her tripping downstairs with an unlikely lightness in a woman of her years. No doubt she went straight to the phone to give the news to Klaus and Hildegard. The pair, I later learnt, were cook and chauffeur to Lady Charlotte Wray, but they did not stop long with her, and the last I heard of him he was Claud Miller and Conservative Mayor of Lewisham. Käthe was with Lady Thorrington until she died.

Now Lady Thorrington came back in, a smile on her face, and closed the door.

"Sherry," said Lady Charlotte.

She said it in a downright, regal way that left no option for refusal, though it was not hers to offer. Lady Thorrington, still in high good humour, went to the decanter and glasses on the cabinet by the window and poured three glasses. The sherry was a brown, dry Amontillado, no more common then than it is today. There was no alternative — it was clearly *their* drink, and very good it was too. When I had taken my glass and sipped it in what I imagined to be the approved manner, I realized that I was seated on one side of the fireplace and that they were seated on the other side, and that both gave every appearance of being about to question me. An inquisition of Ladies! I wished myself a hundred miles from Belgrave Square.

"You find your work at the Foreign Office interesting?" began Lady Charlotte. The Commencement Anodyne. I replied in my earnest, overgrown-schoolboy manner.

"Yes, very interesting. It's such an exciting time to be starting there. Of course, I haven't got to deal with anything of real importance yet." The moment it was out of my mouth I realized where *that* led.

"Only with tiresome old ladies whose business ought to be conducted through the Post Office or the telephone service," said Lady Thorrington with a smile.

"Oh — I'm sorry — of course I didn't mean —"

"Of course you meant it, and quite right too."

We all sipped, to cover my discomfiture.

"No doubt there were others who started with you and who are also on the bottom rung of the ladder," said Lady Charlotte. The Approach Oblique.

"Yes, of course," I murmured. "Several others."

"The Foreign Office, I believe, recruits its young men from all sorts of schools these days," she went on. The Diplomatic Side-Step. "Quite democratic."

"I went to Dulwich," I murmured.

She nodded, as if this confirmed her assessment of the new democratic spirit in the Foreign Office. Indeed, I think I was half-inclined to accept her assessment myself until I saw a tiny twinkle in Lady Thorrington's eye and realized how ridiculous it was. Realized, too, that Lady Thorrington kept her friend as much for her own amusement as anything else.

"Young Wycliffe started there not long ago, I believe."

At last Lady Charlotte had come to the Approach Direct.

"Yes, he did."

"Isn't he some kind of relation of yours?" Lady Thorrington asked her friend. Lady Charlotte gestured dismissively.

"Something. Second cousin twice removed, something of *that* sort. We are all so intermarried that you only count people as related if you actually keep up with them. And as far as the Wycliffes are concerned, my father . . . chose not to."

It was said in a tight-lipped way. I should mention that Lady Charlotte's father was Earl of Bodmin, a generally undistinguished peer, and her husband was Julian Wray, a minor minister in a Baldwin government, a man from whom Lady Charlotte had become more or less semi-detached in the course of her marriage. He had died the previous year, and her mourning was for him. Lady Thorrington's husband had been Ambassador in Vienna at some time in the thirties, and had sent home any number of warning messages to the British government, which it had ignored. His widow's work with Displaced Persons (what we today would call refugees, I suppose — one of the few instances of our language becoming less euphemistic in recent years) was a continuation of his.

"We saw you, in point of fact," she now said.

"I beg your pardon?"

"We saw you and Timothy Wycliffe arrive." She gestured to a corner, where there sat a coffee-cream coloured cat, all soft fur and pugnacious expression. "We were exercising Shaipur in the gardens. We saw you arrive."

The gardens were the fenced-off and locked area in the centre of the Square, exclusive to the Square's residents. There were small trees and shrubs there, providing cover. It was perfect for observing without being observed.

"Ah," I said.

"Is he an especially close friend of yours?" asked Lady Charlotte. The voice was bright, neutral, but the question was loaded.

I had taken my decision.

"Yes, we're very good friends."

"Yet you had not been to his flat before."

I was unable to think of anything to say to that. Did they keep a twenty-four-hour-a-day watch on his flat? Or were they in touch with MI5, who did? After a moment Lady Thorrington took pity on my disconcertment and explained.

"As you were coming along Halkin Street from the Palace we saw that you would have walked straight into the Square if Timothy Wycliffe had not stopped you and pointed to the mews. We deduced from that that you had not been there before."

"You would make very good detectives," I said.

Lady Charlotte was inclined to look affronted, but Lady Thorrington nodded almost complacently.

"Yes, I think we would."

There was a silence, apparently left for me to explain. I explained.

"We have only known each other since we both started working at the Foreign Office. When I said we were friends I meant that we were good friends at work."

"Ah." Lady Charlotte's voice had a ring of satisfaction. She prepared the Thrust Deadly. "Because that young man does have a great many friends."

"I'm sure he does."

"Unsuitable friends."

I sipped my sherry, plucking up courage.

"He has not asked me to advise him on his choice of friends."

"Don't —" began Lady Charlotte, but Lady Thorrington interrupted her.

"Of course you think us interfering old busybodies. And you're quite right. What else is there to be at our ages? The fact is, it's not just us. The Square is beginning to talk. The place is full of people who know his father, and naturally they take an interest in young Timothy."

"For the past week," said Lady Charlotte, her voice sinking to a sort of bass hiss, making her sound like an asthmatic cat, "he has had staying at his flat a young German."

"The war is over," I said.

"I am not referring to the war. I am referring to unnatural vice. To someone of my generation young German boys mean only one thing: that poet chappie and his friend, mixing with the lowest of the low in the bars of Berlin."

"Auden," said Lady Thorrington. "W. H."

I breathed an internal sigh of relief. They seemed to know nothing about Heinz's East German origins.

"I'm too young to know anything about that," I said. "I expect if that side of Berlin survived the Nazis coming to power it must have been flattened in 1945. It is rather hard to imply that young German men should be shunned just because of some poet twenty years ago, isn't it?"

"Of course people would not be talking — even people in Belgravia would not be talking — if the young man were not one of a succession," said Lady Thorrington. "That is what we are so worried about. Young Wycliffe is such a likable young man, or seems so."

"He is."

"Bad blood," said Lady Charlotte. Lady Thorrington shook her head, smiling gently.

"I've always said that there are bad people and bad upbringings, but no such thing as bad blood," she said. "Or good, come to that. What we felt —"

"Yes?"

"— was that perhaps you could give him — not a warning, of course we have no right to give him that — but if you could just tell him that people are talking —"

"I see. Could we be a little more open about this? What exactly are they saying?"

Lady Charlotte clicked her tongue, as if she felt that she had already been more than sufficiently explicit. But Lady Thorrington said: "That Timothy Wycliffe is a homosexual who consorts with extremely dubious young men, and that if he continues to do this openly he will ruin his career in the Foreign Office."

I set down my sherry glass, and thought for a moment. Then I picked my way carefully through this minefield.

"We have just . . . in point of fact . . . been talking about that. And I think I can say . . . that Timothy is aware of the dangers . . . and I would guess too that he realizes that people are talking."

Lady Thorrington nodded, but Lady Charlotte looked most dissatisfied and said: "Is that all you've got to say? Do you mean you haven't warned the silly fellow?"

"Lady Charlotte, Timothy Wycliffe is slightly senior to me in the Foreign Office, and immensely superior to me in experience, worldly wisdom, and almost anything else you care to name. Any warning that could be given I have given. Now what he does is up to him."

"Then can't you do something practical? Find some nice young gel for him?"

I caught once more a glimmer of amusement in Lady Thorrington's eyes, and I was saved from having to reply when she said:

"I imagine there were girls aplenty throwing themselves at him when he was at university. If he didn't get interested then, I don't imagine he will now."

Lady Charlotte shook her head.

"Where did he go to uinversity?" she demanded of me.

"Cambridge, I believe."

"Ah! I knew there was something."

I was mystified at the time, though I realize now that people in the know were already beginning to get suspicious of Cambridge. I should add, to avoid adding further obloquy to that much-maligned university, that Timothy Wycliffe once told me that he was a regularly practising homosexual by the time he was fifteen, at Eton. (Eton, it sometimes seems to me, gets off very lightly from the sort of generalizations that Cambridge falls victim to.) Anyway, nobody could accuse Cambridge of making Timothy Wycliffe a spy, for he never was one.

By now it seemed to me that I had put up with their inquisition as long as I reasonably could be expected to. I finished my sherry and stood up.

"I really must be going. You've been most hospitable."

"Nonsense. We've grilled you unmercifully. But our intentions were at least half-way good. Charlotte is interested in him because he is — remotely — family, and I'm interested in him because I've met him once or twice, at parties and so on, and he seemed an excep-

43

tionally nice and able young man."

"He is."

When I had responded to Lady Charlotte's stately farewell, my hostess followed me down the stairs, and it was she, not Käthe, who let me out. At the door she gave me a grin that was almost girlish as she said:

"You handled that very well."

It was the first compliment I ever received on my tact and diplomacy. In after years, as my political career burgeoned, I received many, so much so that I began thinking of myself as Tact and Diplomacy Proctor — a dull stick, I felt. As I walked down the steps and out into the Square I thought about it, preening myself mildly.

The Belgrave Square of those days was very unlike the place as it is today. Now it is very uniform, spotlessly well-kept, and smells of Tenants' Associations and Keeping Up Property Values. It is all a little unreal, like a film set. Then, as I said earlier, it was a place where genteel shabbiness predominated over discreet smartness: there was a whiff of many different kinds of wealth, though solid, titled, Conservative English wealth still was in the ascendent. As I walked around it and up towards Hyde Park Corner I meditated on the scene I had just played a part in. These people all knew each other, or of each other. Often they were connected in some way with each other: by family or marriage, by business connections, by political activity. They were connected with each other and they protected each other. They formed a tightly knit group which felt that, united, they could take on the world. Or, maybe, rule the world. The scene I had just been a part of at Lady Thorrington's had been an example of them protecting their own.

There was, the more I thought about it, an ironic ambiguity about Tim's position. He was more exposed than he would have been anywhere else in London, because he was surrounded by people of his own kind. On the other hand, those people, for that very reason, were bent on protecting him. I suppose you could say that on balance the situation worked to his advantage: the conduct of his private life never became anything worse than a scandal in Belgravia. Except, of course, briefly, when he was murdered.

4

LORDS A-LEAPING

I have found a way out of my writer's block.

Really it's only an avoidance mechanism, but avoidance is something politicians become good at. I have decided to forget about my doings in the fifties and sixties: my years in industry, my marriage, the four years in the Commons from '62 to '66. Instead I have leapt ahead to my return to the Commons in 1970, the first years of the Heath government, and my first taste of office, after the reshuffle of 1972. I have just been writing about my first days as a junior minister at the Home Office — waxed lyrical, in fact: said that the joy and pride I felt when I was offered the job could only be compared to my elation when my elder son Reggie was born. Have I gone over the top there? Compared the ridiculous with the sublime? From the point of view of me, today — yes I have. But from the point of view of me, then? I fear not. From the first I was always a politician who wanted office, wanted to get things done. And the doing of these political things filled my life quite satisfactorily for many years, though it is true that by the time I left office — was relieved of my office — I was feeling like an old man in a dry month.

Now the writing is coming easily again, and somehow the decision leaves me free to pursue the wraithe of Timothy Wycliffe — who he was, how he lived and how he died.

I know how he died, of course. I know what people in the party say when the subject comes up: "Remember that son of Lord John Wycliffe? Done to death by his boyfriend. Terrible. Tragic." And as often as not they will add: "It only goes to show —" without specifying what. But beyond that I know nothing: simply the bare facts of the death of someone I counted as a friend, someone whose joy in life, frankness, and openmindedness I admired and — I hope — allowed to influence me. Today I got down my *Burke's Peerage* and looked up his father. It's an old one, but it does. Lord John Wycliffe, younger son of the Marquess of Redmond, was given a Life Peerage in 1971 as Baron Edmonton, but this is too late for my *Burke*. He gets in as a younger son, and his children are listed as James (b. 15 Jan. 1925, m. Caroline Weatherby 1950), Timothy (b. 2 Sept. 1927; d. 1956) and Marjorie (b. 4 March 1936). An inch and a half of a line in a reference book — Timothy's life in digest form. Yet somehow Housman could not have made it more pathetic.

I had an appointment at the House of Lords today with Lord Butterworth, who is one of the government's Deputy Whips in the upper house. He got junior office at the same time as I did, and there was a minor matter connected with that time I wanted to talk over. I was told he could see me on Wednesday, today, but that he would be frightfully busy, and I'd have to catch him on the wing in the lobby some time between two and three. Even as plain Jim Butterworth he had been rather a self-important little twit, and it was clear ennoblement had not changed him.

So there I was, soon after two, in Pugin's lovely little lobby, hanging around and exchanging salutations with friends — as often as not ex-ministers like myself, men who, after years of being threatened with the axe, had finally felt it fall. It makes for a cheery yet slightly uneasy camaraderie between us. One of them merrily waved and shouted, "See you here soon, eh?" There have been rumours of a Life Peerage for me, and counterrumours too. The then Prime Minister was known to be displeased when I decided to resign my seat shortly after being relieved of office, thus forcing a by-election in which we did badly.

I don't care much either way. I have more than enough to do, with my business interests, the various worthy bodies I am on the boards of, my memoirs. I would not be an active member of the upper house. Indeed, an active Lord seems to be almost a contradiction in terms.

Though in fact I soon became aware that this was a very busy day indeed for the Lords. People were bustling everywhere, and I kept recognising the faces of people I had believed, and in several cases hoped, had died years ago. Most of them were old, or gave the impression of long disuse. It just had to be one of those days when Bertie Denham was bussing (or rather Rollsing) in decrepit peers from the backwoods to ensure the passing of a particularly unpopular piece of legislation. I had my *Times* with me and managed to turn it to the Parliamentary page. I was right: the Lords were debating the Student Loans question.

And that of course was the burden that was sung by Jim Butterworth when finally he bustled up.

"Peter! Wonderful to see you again! Sorry I can't spare more than a few moments, but you see how it is."

I might have been a constituent whose support he valued but whose company he could dispense with. I felt a pang: how totally our

49

positions had been reversed from the time when I was a Minister and he could be expected to lard any exchanges with a coating of fawn. I suppressed the pang as soon as I felt it: it is a far, far better life that I live now . . .

I put my little problem concerning my early office under Edward Heath, and he confirmed various impressions in my mind. I'll say this about Butterworth: he's a twit, but a twit with a good memory. He was just shifting from foot to foot, preparatory to going about his business of whipping in the noble geriatrics when he hit on an unlucky topic.

"Memoirs going well, old chap?"

His expression said "Please don't tell me," but I was annoyed by the "old chap" which expressed a matiness there certainly never had been between us and I replied: "Not bad, now that I've jumped a few years forward. I'd somehow got hung up on an old friend of mine, Timothy Wycliffe."

He swivelled back to face me, caught on the wing. For the first time I had his full attention.

"Timothy *Wy*cliffe?"

"That's right. Lord John Wycliffe's son. We were at the F.O. together in the early fifties."

"But what on earth are you writing about him for?"

Jim Butterworth's face was contorted, as if with distaste.

"I didn't say I was writing about him. In fact, thinking about him was preventing my writing anything for a time." He wasn't taking it in. It was like talking to a very perturbed brick wall. I added: "What's all the fuss about?"

He spluttered, his face going even redder than normal.

"Well really, old boy, I don't think you're en*tire*ly naive, are you? You know very well where the government stands in the polls at the moment. And if there's one thing that always endangers a Conservative government it's a sex scandal."

That was true, though I am sometimes inclined to wonder, knowing my former colleagues, whether the present government is not more likely to be brought down by a financial rather than a sexual scandal.

"Timothy Wycliffe died over thirty years ago," I protested. "He wasn't an MP, nor even a Conservative at the time I knew him."

"His father was an MP and a minister. You know perfectly well the sort of mud people throw at us whenever there's a scandal in high places. The media pretend to support us, but they go after that sort of thing like pigs after truffles. I'd have thought that you of all people

51

could have seen that that's an affair that is still best kept under wraps."

I shrugged. Jim Butterworth is the sort of person it is hardly worth arguing with. He's like the woman in the Thurber story who was not to be convinced by mere proof. It was his undoing as a junior minister.

"I expect that's where I shall leave it. There's no reason nowadays why anyone except me should be interested in Timothy. I was wondering about his family. I don't remember when his father died."

"Died? He's not dead! He's *here*."

"Here?"

"In the H — Oh my God! Keep your voice down. There he is."

I turned to where he was looking. Coming from the direction of the Chamber, on his way to the Dining Room, was a very old, shrunken peer, walking very uncertainly, and aided along by someone I took to be a fellow peer only marginally less decrepit. I could only see the side of his face, but I had the impression of a strong face now caved in, of a robust body now shrunken and tremulous. I could feel the hackles on the back of my neck rising. I was reminded of Mrs. Alving at the door to the dining room. Like her I shivered and said: "Ghosts!"

"Not at all, old boy. A vote," said Jim

Butterworth, with professional heartlessness. With an abrupt change of emotional key he added: "But you wouldn't really want to upset a fine old man like that by publishing ancient scandals about his son, would you? Think it over, Peter."

I sighed.

"Jim, I have tried to explain to you that I have said nothing at all about publishing." By now I was thoroughly nettled by his dimness and pomposity, so it was probably with malice that I added: "You were at Eton with Timothy, weren't you?"

I had found that out from *Who's Who*. Under "Butterworth, Lord," it had said "b. 20 Jan. 1927; Educ. Eton." He spluttered magnificently at what was common knowledge.

"I say, really old boy — what are you suggesting? I hardly knew the man — Years apart —"

"You were born the same year."

"Different houses. Never mixed in the same set at all."

"He had a very remarkable personality. Immensely likeable. I'm sure you knew *of* him."

By now poor Jim was nearly purple, and puffing. He sank his voice to a mere whisper.

"Well, yes, certainly I knew *of* him. And the fact is that he had a certain — reputation. Don't like speaking ill of the dead, you know:

de mortuis nil . . . desperandum —"

"— *nil nisi bonum —"*

"Right. Exactly. But the fact is, young Wycliffe got in with a set quite early on — a set of older boys. Boys that . . . that the decent chaps wouldn't touch with a bargepole. Of course that meant they protected him — very useful for Timothy. But it was always felt there must be a certain —"

I wondered whether to risk *quid pro quo,* but suggested: "Service offered in return?"

"Ex*act*ly, old boy. Hit the nail on the head. And with the benefit of hindsight, we were obviously right, weren't we?"

"Maybe, maybe. But to get back to what we were talking about: the Wycliffe family."

"Well, of course they're the Redmonds, you must know that. Grandfather was Marquess — and the current man's Tim's cousin. Rather a dim soul, I believe. Never comes *here.*"

That, I suspected, was Jim Butterworth's criterion for dimness in a Lord.

"I meant Tim's immediate family —"

"Did I hear you talking about Timothy Wycliffe."

It was Lord Wratton, a Liberal peer (I suppose he calls himself a Democrat peer nowadays, which sounds even worse than a working one). I had known him as Harry Wratton in the House, a very hard-working and well-liked Liberal MP who had been forced to resign during a long illness. I was pleased to see he now looked healthy enough, for I had always got on well with him, in that across-the-floor way that precludes any real intimacy or confidence.

Jim Butterworth shot me a furious glance that said "*Now* look what you've done," and bustled away. He had remembered that he was busy.

"You weren't at Eton with Tim, were you, Harry?" I asked, turning to him with one of those resigned smiles that showed that we both knew Jim Butterworth to be an ass.

"Good Lord, no. Well above my station, I'm glad to say. That particular sort of misery is reserved for the well-heeled. No, I knew him at home. The Wycliffes' home was in Bristol then, you know. Very substantial, inclining to the grand, and actually running to a butler, who doubled butling with Air Raid Precaution work — all this only a few hundred yards from our street of semi-detacheds."

"Ah! I'd always assumed, somehow, that they had some minor country house somewhere or other. I suppose Bristol was where Lord John's parliamentary seat was."

"That's right — that was the seat he lost in '45. Though the home wasn't actually *in* the constituency, which didn't have anything grand enough — still, it was near enough to pass muster. We somehow fell in with each other in vacation time, Tim and me."

"How?"

Harry Wratton frowned.

"Do you know, I can't remember. Some perfectly natural way, because it was only after we'd known each other for some time that I realized I ought to be rather impressed by the fact that he was an Etonian. In fact it never struck me until much later that friendships between Etonians and a gang of grammar-school lads just didn't happen as a general rule."

"When was this?"

"Right at the beginning of the war. We were just about into our teens, I remember that, but a lot of the kids in our gang were younger. It was the time when all the children were spotting spies — anyone with a foreign accent or pince-nez glasses was marked down right away, and sometimes tracked for hours. I expect most of them were Jews, poor sods. Timothy changed all that. He announced that we were looking for Fifth Columnists."

"That was rather inventive," I said, the period suddenly very vivid in my mind. "In Dulwich we'd heard the term, but I'm not at all sure that we knew what it meant. We stuck with boring old spies."

"Timothy explained it to us. He said it was the most apparently respectable and upright who were Fifth Columnists, and they were devoted to undermining the war effort and national morale by subtly spreading gloom and despondency, preparing the way for a German occupation. It was great fun — all the local pillars of the community were under suspicion, and at least it took some of the heat off the poor guys with the pince-nez and funny accents."

"That was just like Timothy. He always came up with the unexpected."

"That's right. And always such fun. The other times, when he wasn't around, what I remember is the poor food, the bombs, my father being away in North Africa. But when Timothy was around all I can remember is the fun."

"He never, er, at that stage —"

"The homosexuality thing? No. I had no idea until long after — not till I worked in London at Liberal HQ in the mid-fifties. Oh no, he never brought that home with him."

"You're assuming it started at Eton?"

"Well, it's pretty bloody probable, isn't it?" He grinned at me, and I realized that now I was an ex-minister and he was practically an ex-politician we could become friends, in a way that would never have been possible before.

"Anyway, I overheard most of what that prat Butterworth was saying. When he sinks his voice to a whisper he can be heard all over the Chamber. Don't let him talk about Tim as if he were a problem or a scandal. He was a joy." He started to move away. "Sorry to have interrupted. Hope I didn't make him scurry away before you got what you wanted."

"No wait, Harry. I was asking Jim, but you can probably tell me. There was a brother and a sister, wasn't there?"

He pondered.

"Let's see. Tim was a younger son, like his father. There was just the one elder brother, and he certainly didn't mix with us. I'm trying to recall any impression of him. . . . A little stiff, I think, formal, certainly not as bright as Tim. . . . I think maybe Tim's outgoingness embarrassed him or bothered him. I certainly don't remember them as being close."

"And the sister?"

"Ah, that was different. Marjorie — but she wasn't a Marjorie at all. I always think of Marjories as being dull, conventional girls. This one was a kid sister, years younger, and the apple of Tim's eye. Of course she idolised him. She was one of our gang almost from the start. A real charmer, and very bright."

"So you were in and out of each other's houses?"

"We-ell, it wasn't quite like that. Tim's wasn't the sort of house kids would be in and out of. Or maybe we just didn't have the confidence to treat it like that."

"You felt socially inadequate?"

"Certainly Tim never made us feel that. But deep down we must have known we were. I mean, say the subject of homosexuality *had* come up. The fact is, we probably would have gawped and said, 'Yer what?' There are millions of ways of revealing gaucheness, and I should think we displayed all of them."

"What about the mother?"

Harry Wratton wrinkled his forehead again.

"Do you know I hardly remember her. Certainly not forbidding, as the father inevitably was — being a lord, and an MP, and very much a local figure. But she — the mother — was not particularly warm or welcoming. . . . Somehow I have the impression of someone who wasn't really *there*. . . . Certainly her children, or the two younger ones, were infinitely more vital than she was herself."

"How long did all this last?"

"Oh — three or four years. As long as the war. Things were beginning to draw us apart by then. It was just a holiday friendship in any case — it had to be renewed every time the schools broke up. Then Sir John lost his seat in the 1945 election, the family moved, and that was that. I imagine Timothy did his national service about that time. So we never managed to make contact again. But I still look back on him with affection. He was a wonderful person — so enthusiastic, so alive."

He'd used the word I had used. The saddest possible word.

"Any idea what happened to the brother and sister?"

"No idea at all. . . . Wait a minute, though. The sister married an artist fellow. One read about him now and then on the arts pages. No, not an artist, a sculptor. That would be decades ago — heaven knows if they're still married. What was the name? Foreign name, I know. Maybe Jewish . . . Knopfmeyer? Would that be it? Name mean anything to you?"

I shook my head.

"I've never been much good on the visual arts."

Nor on most of the other arts, I'm afraid, though my son Reggie at one stage tried to civilise me, and Jeremy is continuing the process. I'm an old-fashioned books man, I think.

"Well, I think it's a name people know," Wratton continued, "people who are into sculpture. . . . Anyway, why this interest in Timothy all of a sudden? I mean, he was a marvellous person, but why *now?*"

"I want to find out what happened to him."

"He was murdered by one of his boyfriends. Everyone knows that."

"How do they know? Was there a trial?"

"Oh no. I would have remembered if there had been. I think the boy left the country — got away entirely."

I nodded. Maybe that was why I had so few memories of the case — there had been no trial. I didn't remark, as a former Home Office Minister, that according to him "everyone knew" something that had never been tested in court.

When I got home I idly took down the telephone directory and looked up the name Knopfmeyer. There were three. One was Knopfmeyer, M, and her address made my heart stop. She lived at 4 Craven Court Mews.

5

A MEAL in COVENT GARDEN

I have not mentioned Elspeth Honeybourne, my research assistant for the writing of my memoirs. She was recommended — almost passed on — to me by Raymond Hadleigh, a cabinet minister on whom the Prime Ministerial axe had fallen in 1984, and who wrote his memoirs immediately afterwards. Elspeth is a treasure: efficient, versatile, enthusiastic. She comes to my home one day a week to put my papers in order for whatever topic I happen to be dealing with at that time, and for the rest of the week she hovers around in libraries, mainly the London Library and the British Library's newspaper section in North London somewhere. Jeremy pretends to believe that she has ambitions to be the second Mrs. Proctor, even Lady Proctor, but I know that is not the case: she has what cant phraseology calls a "stable relationship" with a solicitor in South London.

Elspeth is happy now that I've hopped to

a point where I have a position, however lowly, in government. It gives her much more to go on. She has a scrapbook which Ann started keeping soon after we were married, but she supplements this from the sort of newspapers we never took. From 1972 onwards I was answering questions in the House, putting out statements on this and that, making the odd formal speech, and she can pick them all up in national and local newspaper reports. (How exciting I found all that sort of thing then, how stale and routine it all seems now!) I also gave her, last week, the name of Timothy Wycliffe and the year of his death, and asked her to pick up anything she could on it.

Today she bustled in, all plump and smiling, refused a cup of coffee (wisely, for I would have had to make it myself, it being my Filipino couple's day off), and then started setting out a great wad of photocopies on the lead-up to the Sunningdale Agreement on Northern Ireland, in which well-intentioned but abortive initiative I played a small part. We went through them, I suggested one or two further avenues of enquiry, and when we were finished she opened her briefcase again.

"Oh — the Timothy Wycliffe affair."

"The murder."

"That's right. Sorry — did I sound heartless? I didn't mean to. I thought it might be worthwhile in this case to get facsimile copies of some of the newspapers for the relevant dates. You'll see why."

She bustled out again, leaving a wad of complete facsimile newspapers and a smaller wad of xeroxed items from other newspapers. My curiosity pricked, I took up the top newspaper, a *Daily Telegraph*. I immediately saw what she meant.

GAITSKELL ATTACKS SUEZ "ADVENTURE"

"Treason" say Tory MPs

Timothy Wycliffe had been murdered at the height of the Suez crisis.

I remember talking to a class of intelligent eighteen-year-olds when I was Minister of Education. I mentioned the Suez crisis, and was met with completely blank looks. I explained that this was when Britain and France, on a spurious excuse, invaded Egypt to gain control of the Suez Canal, which Colonel Nasser had nationalised. They were halted by U.S. opposition and outraged world opinion. Then I got some intelligent comparisons with the Falklands invasion. But it is interesting that Suez has not entered the folk imagination, as the Second World War has. For someone of my generation it is the watershed, *the* political event, from which all else has followed.

If I had remembered that, of course, I would have realized why the murder had had so little impact on me at the time, and why it had aroused so little interest in the newspapers. As I flicked through them one after another I found what I expected: page after page about the crisis, the storms in Parliament, the bombing of Egyptian air bases, the landing of French and British troops in the Suez zone, the reactions of the international great and good. Coverage of Timothy's death was minimal, and perhaps the report of it in the *Telegraph* can be taken for all.

MINISTER'S SON KILLED

Police confirmed last night that the man found battered to death in a flat in Belgravia was Timothy Wycliffe, son of the Minister of Planning and Public Works, Lord John Wycliffe.

In the days that followed there was nothing more of substance on the murder until the day that the Suez invasion was halted, when again the newspapers contained little except that story, as the inquest and the recriminations began. Several of them, though, did have a tiny item on the murder, of which one may

65

again quote the *Telegraph* as typical.

MAN SOUGHT IN MINISTER'S SON'S KILLING

Police have issued the name of a man they wish to interview in connection with the killing of Timothy Wycliffe, son of the Minister of Planning and Public Works. He is Andrew Forbes, an unemployed electrician, of Peckham.

I sat for some time, thinking. Now I had a name for the young man who, according to Harry Wratton, had left the country after the murder of Timothy. I was beginning to doubt everything anybody told me about the case because they all, like me, would have been so involved with the Suez invasion that they would have taken in very little at the time. Suez was different. Young people may read about it in history books, but they will never understand the atmosphere of those weeks. Suez was the one issue in our postwar history that left no one indifferent, whatever their politics.

However Harry Wratton did not seem to have got that bit wrong. When I sorted through Elspeth Honeybourne's little pile of xeroxed sheets (which mostly contained alternative versions of the two news items I've just quoted), I found one small item in a South

66

London newspaper saying that the police feared that the man they wanted to question in connection with the murder of Timothy Wycliffe had left the country. They would be investigating the possibility of extradition, but they feared that he had gone to Spain, with which country Britain had no extradition treaty.

And that — so far as Elspeth Honeybourne had gone — was the end of the matter in the British press.

Andrew Forbes. I tried to remember whether that was one of Timothy's boyfriends I had met. I did get introduced to them now and again, at the theatre or opera, in restaurants, or when they met him from the Foreign Office after work. There had been one young man who made terrible scenes at the F.O. for a whole week, and I'd been the one deputed to deal with him. Tact and Diplomacy Proctor, in an early manifestation. The only other boyfriend I had more than casual words with was a man called Derek Wicklow. I remember him because of the circumstances of our one meeting, and because he later became governor of one of our last colonies — St. Helena or Mauritius or some such place — and I remember thinking that he must have become a whole lot more discreet in his conduct since I knew him.

We met at a restaurant in Covent Garden, long gone now, called Les Tuileries — met, in fact, at the door. It was evening time, and I was with a very pushy girl called Veronica something-or-other. She was a sort of Edwina Currie figure, intent on pushing her way ahead in politics, and since I was by then making some sort of a name with the London Young Conservatives I was a minor figure on her hit list. (She never did get a parliamentary seat, by the way, let alone become Prime Minister. She married a millionaire who gave her two children and then sensibly left her, though I'm sure she stung him for enormous alimony.) When Timothy and Derek Wicklow turned up at the door to Les Tuileries at the same time as us, having failed to get standing tickets for Callas in *Norma*, I think I was a bit relieved, and jumped at Tim's suggestion that we should make a foursome. A couple of hours' verbal battering by the intense and single-minded Veronica was not an enticing prospect.

The topic of Callas lasted us through the process of ordering and waiting for the soup. Timothy had seen her first Norma and had been hoping to see her with the new Adalgisa. It was fairly typical of Timothy that he had forgotten when the first day of the new booking period was, and had found all the tickets gone by the time he remembered. Derek Wicklow had seen her in the Verona Arena on a holiday with his parents. I had just about heard of her. I doubt whether Veronica had. There was no way the topic was going to last into the soup course — people still ate soup then — because she was a single issue person (I wonder what that single issue is today: monetarism? the environment? the ordination of women?) and she was determined at the first lull in the talking to turn the topic to politics.

"*Do* you feel this government's really got a grip of things?" she asked suddenly of me, *à propros* of nothing. She had turned to me so as totally to exclude the others. I should say that at the time of this encounter Churchill had been Prime Minister again for something like two years.

"Oh — ah — well, of course they're going cautiously because —"

"But that's not what we expected of Winnie, is it? I mean, the British people didn't elect him to be *cautious*. They expected him to weigh in and knock down all those damned Socialist regulations. . . ."

I will give no more than a specimen of Veronica's conversation. It was in the steam-roller style (one to which I've become accustomed during my years in the Cabinet), and it was certainly not entertaining. As she beavered on I became aware that Timothy was right-handed and Derek was left-handed, and that their unoccupied hands were together under the table. It says something for my increased sophistication by this time that I was amused as well as disconcerted. Veronica had certainly not noticed. She was one of those people who would never notice anything about other people unless it was shoved in her face. The whole situation — Veronica droning away like a dentist's drill, the pair opposite spooning, her quite oblivious of it — was exquisitely ludicrous.

". . . we expected so much *more*," she concluded. "It makes you wonder whether he's really in con*trol*."

"He's in control," said Timothy, drawling more than was his wont. "The thing you're forgetting about Churchill is that he's not really a Tory."

This stopped Veronica in her tracks. I suspected that she had no knowledge of history. Timothy explained.

"He was a Liberal for the first twenty years of this century. In many ways he still thinks like a Liberal — social affairs, for instance. He's an old-fashioned Conservative where the Empire, God bless it, is concerned, but if you're expecting him to abolish the National Health Service, forget it: it just isn't going to happen. . . . Golly, how *bored* I am with politics."

"Timothy's father is in the Cabinet," I explained. "He's had his fill of politics over the years."

"In the Cabinet?" said Veronica with drill-like intensity and turning to him. "What's your name? Sorry, I didn't catch it."

"Wycliffe. Timothy Wycliffe."

"*Wy*cliffe! Oh, but I must tell you I think your father's doing an absolutely superb job —" she bent forward, nearly knocking a plate of lamb chops from the waiter's hand. Timothy managed a tiny amused smile. He knew and I knew that the Minister of Planning and Public Works had a job so humdrum that there was no way anyone could make a superb job of it. Veronica now forgot about me and gave her entire attention to Timothy, though not to the extent of giving him much chance to reply. She was quite oblivious, I noticed, when Timothy and Derek disengaged their hands to eat their meal, and oblivious too to the looks Timothy gave me that said as plainly as words: "Help!"

There was little help I could give. Veronica was one of those unstoppable forces. However after she had gone on for some minutes in effusive praise of Timothy's father it did seem to occur to her — she was not very bright

71

— that her praise was eliciting little response, and was more than a little inconsistent with her former verdict that the government lacked grip. Accordingly she switched her tack.

"I suppose you're politically active yourself?"

It was said in an accusatory tone, as if it was the duty of all right-minded people. In the subsequent decade a young woman of Veronica's stamp would probably have said "sexually active" in much the same tone of voice.

"Good Lord, no. Not at all."

"But really you should be! There's any number of really vital and active organisations that you could give a hand to. The Young Conservatives are absolutely the most forward-looking political group in the country at the moment."

"I'm sure. But I doubt if I am young enough or Conservative enough for them."

"Oh, nonsense. You don't even have to be particularly political. For a lot of people it's mainly social — dances, parties, practically a marriage bureau!" She was getting quite roguish, in a galumphing kind of way that made me shudder. "It really is a tremendous hoot, I can assure you!"

"That's what I'm afraid of," murmured Timothy.

"No, really, you've got the wrong idea entirely." Veronica had shown a surprising facility in coping with lamb chops and wielding her verbal battering ram simultaneously. Now she was finished and doubly intimidating, leaning forward over the table and fixing Timothy with her basilisk eyes. "Look, the Kensington Y.C.s are having this dance next Saturday. Why don't you come along as my guest?"

It was Derek Wicklow, resourcefully, who brought Timothy the aid I had been unable to supply. He too leaned forward, putting his hand over Timothy's and speaking, not loudly but distinctly, so that he could be heard at the tables next to ours.

"Look, ducky, Timothy is fucking me, right? So you're just not in with a chance."

Her face was a picture. Her lower jaw literally dropped open, she blinked, spluttered. At last she managed to say, "For God's sake!" jumped up from the table, and scuttled from the restaurant as if she had just been told one of us had leprosy.

We looked at each other, waited till the door slammed, and then burst out all three into uncontrollable laughter, holding our sides, our heads hitting the table as fresh waves of merriment engulfed us. I was dimly conscious of people at the adjacent table studying their plates as if they were runic tablets, then hurrying up their eating, but I only really surfaced when I became conscious of a waiter at my elbow. He murmured:

"The young lady's dessert?"

"Me, me," said Timothy. "I'm a snapper-up of unconsidered trifles."

The rest of the meal was wholly merry, with imitations of Veronica, periodically renewed laughter, and frequent demands to know where on *earth* I had picked her up. It is a measure of my greater sophistication that by this time I could participate in it, though I seem to remember saying at one point, "What an absolutely marvellous way of getting rid of her!" for the benefit of the adjoining tables, hoping they would believe it was no more than that. More sophisticated, but still craven, a modern person would judge, though I would remind them that homosexual acts were still illegal at that time. Eventually we rolled out into Covent Garden, still laughing, and finding it was interval time at the opera. Tim and Derek declared that they were going to infiltrate the standers and see the rest of Callas and Simionato's performance. I expect they managed it.

Looking back, that is one of my happiest memories of Timothy. He had this wonderful way of pricking pomposity, knocking down pretension, derailing the one-track minded. It seemed that he had managed to pass it on, at least temporarily, to Derek Wicklow. I suspect it was that night in Les Tuileries that gave me a healthy dislike of pushy people — though naturally, being in politics, I have had to put up with a great number of them over the years. Ann, whom I married in 1959, was a very different type.

When I had finished going through Elspeth Honeybourne's collection of snippets I — on an impulse, but one that was always going to come sooner or later — took down the telephone directory again and found the number for Knopfmeyer, M.

"Three-one-oh, four-three-seven-two."

The voice was clear, civilised, with just a trace of that upper-class drawl that Timothy sometimes affected for comic purposes.

"Is that — er — Marjorie Knopfmeyer?"

"It is."

"This is going to sound a bit odd. My name is Peter Proctor —"

"Oh, yes — the ex-minister for whatever-it-was."

The fact that she showed no surprise at being rung up out of the blue by an ex-cabinet minister told me that this was indeed Timothy's sister: she had mingled in cabinet-minister circles all her life.

75

"Minister for all sorts of things in my time," I admitted.

"I thought I recognised your voice. It's funny how top politicians become almost family friends through television these days, isn't it? Or personal enemies. It wasn't like that when my father was in the Cabinet."

"It soon passes though. People pass me in the street and frown slightly, trying to remember who I am."

"Weren't you a friend of Timothy's at one time?"

"Yes, I was. I'm glad you mentioned him. As I say, this is going to sound odd. You see, I'm writing my memoirs —"

"Oh God! Poor old you! Why are political memoirs considered mandatory these days? They're always so tedious. I was forced to read Jim Prior's one wet weekend at a friend's and it was like wading through sump oil."

"Don't sap my confidence any further. The fact is, I got stuck in the fifties, and I think the reason is I feel a sort of guilt at the thought of Timothy's death. Not because I had anything to do with it, but because I knew him, liked him so well, and yet his death made so little impression on me."

"Suez," said Marjorie Knopfmeyer promptly. "Everyone says the same. I remember it so horribly well: it was like being in two night mares simultaneously."

"Yes, I've realized that must be the reason. Look, I believe you and he were close —?"

"We were. He was just the brother every girl would want to have. Do you want to talk about him?"

"Well, yes — oddly enough I would like to. I somehow feel it might — exorcise the memories, or remove the block."

"No need to explain. I still, now and then, meet people who feel they want to talk about Tim. He was the sort of person who affected people that way. Why don't you come to dinner?"

"That would be ideal, if it's not too much trouble."

"I suppose you're very busy?"

"Not at all. You must know that ex-cabinet ministers are like yesterday's newspapers."

"What about Thursday?"

"Fine."

"Say seven thirty. I look forward to it."

I put the phone down, with an odd lift of the heart at the thought of eating dinner with Tim's sister.

6

The *LITTLE SISTER*

Belgrave Square, as I said earlier, is a shadow of its former self as far as character and atmosphere go: uniform, sleek, bland. Inevitably it smells of wealth, but not of very interesting wealth. I was ten minutes early for my dinner with Marjorie Wycliffe, or Marjorie Knopfmeyer rather, so I paid off my taxi in the Square itself and walked around it in the twilight. Lady Thorrington's house had now an opaque, ungiving presence, and I saw from a tiny plaque that it was the office of a finance company. Embassies abounded, prestige offices of this and that. Probably only the Duke of Westminster can afford to live there any longer. It is not, now, a square with much interest attached to it.

Away from the Square itself there is still some style, however, and in the various little mews there is character and atmosphere aplenty. If I had not been remembering so intensely those encounters with Tim I might have had trouble finding Craven Court Mews, for I only went to his flat two or three times, but as it was I found my way there almost without thinking. It was now brightly painted, trim, almost jolly. I rang the bell of the street door and immediately heard steps clattering down the stairs.

"Hello, I'm Marjorie Knopfmeyer. Good of you to come."

She smiled, held out her hand, then led the way up the stairs. She was a big, untidy woman with no pretensions to fashion, in a purple dress with a shawl around her shoulders. What seized me as soon as we got into the light of the sitting room, however, was the realization that she had Tim's charm — a version of it, rather: more feminine, perhaps less brilliant, but a charm that vividly brought Tim himself to my mind. It was there in the smile, the warmth, the informality, the effortless way I was made to feel wanted and welcome.

"Could you be an angel and fix yourself a drink?" she said, waving towards a cabinet. "There are one or two things I have to do in the kitchen."

The bottles were not from a wine merchant's: they were supermarket bottles, with the price labels still on. Where, I wondered, were the supermarkets for Belgravia? Victoria, perhaps? The King's Road? I poured myself a sherry from a standard label bottle, good but not distinguished. Then I looked around the room.

There were still things that I remembered: the glass-topped table edged in rosewood, the escritoire. Most of it, however, was new, and bore the imprint of a life in the art world. There were two largish pictures — a Paul Klee and a Lucien Freud (I did not recognise them, I should say, but looked at the signatures). There were also several watercolours. There was just one piece of sculpture, on a small table under the window: a long-legged bird, like a stork, bending forward and somehow surveying the world quizzically. It was rough, jagged, and gave an impression of human vitality.

"Do you like it?"

Marjorie was standing over by the cabinet, pouring herself a weak gin and tonic.

"Yes, very much."

"Ferdy's. I don't surround myself with memories, it's unhealthy, but I have that piece here and one or two others in Gloucestershire. He gave me that piece explicitly — didn't just leave it to me — because I said it reminded me of him — I don't know why: a sort of humorous disengagement, perhaps. It's all too easy to drown yourself in memories, isn't it? . . . I suppose you remember this room?"

"Yes, though I wasn't often here. I remember this table, and the escritoire . . ." I paused. "Oh yes, and I think I remember that vase. Delft, isn't it?"

I pointed to a small, delicate blue-and-white piece on the cabinet, and as I did so I noticed that Marjorie flinched.

"Yes, that was Tim's."

"I seem to remember it from one of my later visits. I suppose he acquired it. I wouldn't have thought it his kind of thing."

"My mother gave it to him. No, not really his taste . . ." She drank from her gin, a hefty gulp. "If you go close you'll see that it's been repaired. It was smashed the night he died. That's the thing I keep to remember Tim by."

She walked over to the quizzical bird, and I had a sudden stab of realization how much it cost her to talk about Tim's death, even after all these years. This was not sisterly feeling, this was love. She changed the subject.

"Ferdy had charm too. I suppose I could never have married a man who didn't — not after growing up with Tim. Ferdy's was more raffish, he was more of a card, but he was like Tim in making people love him."

"He wasn't English, was he?"

"Oh no. He gets into the books on British sculpture — which is right in a way, because he has to go somewhere, and he was never quite of that stature where nationality becomes unimportant. But he wasn't in the least English. His family were Polish Jews who moved to Germany in the twenties. Ferdy was born in Leipzig. At least they realized their mistake early on, but when they moved, in 1932, it was to Czechoslovakia. They came to Britain in 1937, when Ferdy was in his teens. They'd had money, but by then much of it was gone. I met him when I was twenty-one, soon after Tim died. We lived a racketty, hand-to-mouth existence, but a good one. . . . I miss him horribly."

"You didn't live here?"

"Good Lord, no. We could never have afforded to. I let it out, so it provided a regular income for us over the years. Since he died I've come here occasionally, when it's been vacant, just for a change of scene. I've been here two years now — too long: I'm not a metropolitan person, and all the friends I have here are the wrong sort. I'm longing to get back to Gloucestershire, and I will in a few weeks. I really should sell both places. They both have painful memories. But I'm too old to start afresh, and the children would certainly hate it if I sold the cottage in Barndene. . . . Look, I'll serve the soup and you can start in on what you want to know."

Over the soup, which was onion, and very

pungent, I said:

"You were close to Tim, weren't you?"

"I loved him."

"Close right up to the end?"

She grimaced a little, as if at some painful thought.

"As I say, I prefer to think that I *loved* him, rather than that we were close. I *felt* close to him, but that doesn't mean I saw him all that often. That's one of the things that always nags at the back of my mind: I loved him, he did so much for me, so why didn't I make sure I saw more of him in that last year of his life?"

"You were in London?"

"Yes." She grinned at me mischievously. "Don't laugh — I did the Season!"

I raised my eyebrows at her, and we laughed together.

"Well, I suppose girls like you did in the fifties. Do still, come to that, though I'm glad to say my daughter never wanted to."

"When I did it we were still curtseying to the Queen. Can you imagine it? Poor woman — the boredom of it! No wonder she did away with it all. . . . To be fair to myself, I didn't intend to. I wanted to go straight from school to art school . . . The watercolours are mine, by the way. I have a small reputation in a limited circle, but I do sell my work."

"Why did you change your mind?"

"Mummy — she was very tradition minded. Certain things were done and certain other things were not done. I don't suppose that would have decided me, but she was ill, much more ill, in fact, than we realized. So when I'd got some A-levels I took a year off school, spent a lot of time with her, and in spring I did the Season and curtseyed to Her Majesty and the Duke . . . It seems an age ago!"

"Where were you living then?"

"We had a house in Kensington, and another in the constituency. My father got back to the Commons in 1950, for another West Country constituency — in what is now Avon. Actually he tried to get hold of this place."

"This flat? From Tim?"

"That's right. Tim inherited it about the time my father got back to Westminster. Daddy said it was much too expensive for a young man in his position, sky-high rates and all that, but that it was just right for an MP to spend the working week in. In a way he was right, but I think underneath he was peeved because Aunt Julie hadn't thought of this and left it to him. Anyway Tim turned him down flat, and Tim could be very stubborn when he liked. So we had the house in Kensington, and that's where I did the Season from."

I finished my soup, and putting down my spoon I said, "I haven't got any impression of your mother." Marjorie nodded, pushing back a strand of grey hair.

"No . . . Mummy is difficult to explain." She collected up the soup plates and soon came back with a large, steaming casserole. "Would you pour the wine? This is Lancashire hot-pot. A bit basic, but I don't like dinner parties where the hostess is forever flitting backwards and forwards to the kitchen. With Ferdy stopping work at unpredictable hours of the day and needing feeding there and then I developed a repertoire of meals that could just sit in the oven waiting for him."

"Yes — Ann had the same problem. Not many points of resemblance between artists and MPs, but that's one."

"Did your wife like the traditional Tory MP's wife's role?"

I could be honest with someone of my generation.

"Yes, she did rather. These days one has to be apologetic about that, but she did — at least she liked being a full-time mother, and she regarded the constituency work as being a pleasant few hours' change from the domestic role." I thought, and then added: "At least if she changed her mind about that she never told me."

Marjorie nodded.

"You asked about my mother. The thing about Mummy was that she gave the impression that she was semi-detached, not quite with you. She had a vaguely benign air, but she seemed cocooned in some other world of her own. The constituency people would be talking to her about the rates bill or the price of school blazers and suddenly her words of agreement or sympathy wouldn't quite gell with what they were saying. It got worse as she got older, and used to irritate my father to hell."

"Wasn't she close to her children?"

"She and I were. I never went away to school — she insisted on that. It's different with boys, isn't it? James and Tim went away to prep school when they were seven. She loved them, and they her, but even before that there'd been a nanny, of course, so it could never be what ordinary people would call close. . . . It's unnatural, don't you think, the upper-class way with children? Just too cold. I made sure I kept our two with us."

"Yes, we did too." I glanced at the cabinet, and ventured to bring up the vase again. "You said that vase was a present from your mother to Tim."

She nodded, her eyes slightly wet.

"Yes, she did that in the last year of her

life: went around giving people little unexpected presents — things of her own she
wanted them to have. As if she knew that her
hold on their memories would be as frail as
her hold on life. That's why after the . . .
after Tim died I had it repaired. It was shattered in the . . . attack on him. Now it's part
of my memories of him and her."

"Did you inherit this flat after Tim's
death?"

"Yes. Apart from several bequests to friends
he left everything to me."

"Was the will made shortly before he died?"

"Not particularly . . . Oh, you mean did
he half expect to die as he did? No, I'm sure
he didn't."

"I just wondered whether he had recently
acquired a boyfriend who was particularly violent, and he thought he should put his affairs
in order."

"No, the will was made in 1953. . . ." She
began crumbling her bread. "I met him, you
know."

"Who? The boy who —?"

"Killed him. Yes. I said I met Tim very
little in the last year, and that's true. Oh, of
course we were together about the time of
Mummy's death, which was July, but naturally we weren't talking much about *him*. But
one time that year when I did meet him, he

was with that — that creature."

"Tell me about him."

She swallowed, put her plate aside, and thought.

"I call him a creature, and yet I didn't dislike him at the time. It must have been June, before Mummy died, because I'd been to a ball at the Ritz — predictably dire. I seem to have spent that entire spring and summer escaping from crushingly boring events like that. There were three or four of us who had come away for a bit and drifted along Piccadilly. I remember the air still had a twilight feel to it, so it can't have been too late. And suddenly there was Tim and this man Andy Forbes. He introduced me, of course, but I didn't remember him until the police showed me a picture of him."

"What was he like?"

"Physically? He was about twenty-one or -two, well-built, rather basically dressed. Pretty much what you'd expect of a young man who was an electrician, and from the provinces."

"Unemployed electrician it said in the papers."

"Right. Otherwise my impression was that he was straightforward, not too well educated, rather embarrassed, but fond of Tim. End of impression, I'm afraid."

"What did you talk about?"

"Oh, Tim and I talked about the awfulness of doing the Season, about Mummy's health, whether Daddy was being kind to her — he was, on the whole, but you couldn't bank on it. Naturally Andy Forbes didn't have much to say on those subjects, which is probably why I didn't get any strong impression of him."

"What had they been doing?"

"Been to a John Wayne film, I think. Not to a gay club, I'm sure. Andy Forbes didn't look at all a gay club sort of person. Did they have them then?"

I shrugged and spread out my hands and we both laughed.

"Did you ever meet any of his other boyfriends?"

"A fair number. There had been a time, a year or two earlier, when I was backwards and forwards to his flat. Some I liked, some I wasn't keen on — just as you'd expect, because he had a pretty motley assortment of friends. Tim was infinitely tolerant."

"There was no common denominator?"

"No, none at all. I certainly didn't get the impression he went for the tough, brutal kind."

"No, I didn't either. Though . . ." I stopped myself. A memory had come into my head that I didn't want to tell Marjorie about. I amended it to: "though I only met a few of them. He was very promiscuous, I know that."

"Yes, he was. Homosexuals were then, weren't they? I mean, people like Britten and Pears may have *seemed* to have something like a marriage, but they still hopped into bed with anything that offered. I don't know why it was like that. Since it was against the law you'd have thought that would have been more dangerous, make you more open to blackmail."

"A taste for living dangerously?" I hazarded. "Dancing on the volcano's edge?"

"You may be right. But I never got the impression that Tim had any sort of death wish, did you?"

"Not at all," I said firmly. "He loved life, and wanted to go on living it."

"Yes, I agree. Anyway, I'm not in the business of judging other people's way of life."

"Absolutely not."

"That was Tim's, and as far as I could see he got a lot of pleasure out of it."

"Right up to the time he died?" I wondered. "I didn't see much of him in his last year either."

"Did you not? I didn't realize that."

"I left the F.O. and went to work for Imperial Chemical Industries."

"Ah. Well, as far as I know he did. I don't

think there was any change in his life-style. Actually the last time I saw him he was troubled, but it wasn't anything personal."

"When was this?"

"Just two days before he died. I mentioned the meeting with Andy Forbes, and then Mummy's death. I don't remember any real meeting with him between the funeral and that last time — any meeting when we could really talk. I started at the Slade in September — rather against Daddy's wishes — and I was taken up with the new life, new friends. Then came Suez. It took something to make art students politically active in those days, but Suez did it."

"Yes. I was thinking the other day that was the one thing since the war that involved just everyone."

"That's right. Which side were you on?"

She was looking at me with sharp, intelligent eyes. I laughed, a bit shamefaced.

"I was a wobbler. I knew it was wrong, but I was too much of a party man to stand up and say so. The story of my life. I expect if it had been a rip-roaring success I'd have convinced myself by now that I was for it all along."

"I was against it, of course. Almost all young people were. When I met Tim I was in some sort of ragged procession on the way from the

Houses of Parliament to a big meeting in Trafalgar Square. He was walking down Whitehall — on the way from the Admiralty or somewhere. I was on some sort of high, I think — you know how *tense* we all were then — and I dropped out of the march and ran over to him. I started shouting at him 'Why don't you resign? When are you going to stop this mad government killing people?' — God, how embarrassing to remember that now!"

"We all did pretty silly things at that time." She laughed.

"Except you, apparently. I'm sure you wobbled very discreetly."

"What did Tim do?"

"He took me by the arms, stopped me waving my fists, and said very quietly: 'Stop behaving like a political harridan and start behaving like my sister.' It got through almost at once and I felt very ashamed. Then he said: 'Yes, I agree I can't stay at the F.O. after this. But this isn't the time to go. And when I go I'll go quietly. You're making your protest over this. You're quite right to. I'm not a free agent, though. I'll be making my stand over something else.' Then he kissed me, said 'Love you,' and went on down Whitehall. I suppose I went on up to the meeting in Trafalgar Square — I really don't remember. There were so many meetings at that time."

"And that was the last time you saw him?"

"Yes. James spoke to him on the phone next day, but none of us ever saw him again."

"What did your brother speak to him about?"

"The family was in a bit of a flap, afraid that he was going to do something that would embarrass my father. Not that *I* was — that was exactly what I wanted him to do. Anyway James phoned him, and Tim said pretty much what he had said to me: that it would be wrong to make a futile gesture while British troops were involved. I'd told them that's what he felt, but Tim reassured them. Daddy was Minister of Planning and Public Works at the time — not a high-profile job, but high enough for it to have been an embarrassment to the government if Tim had resigned from the F.O. and talked to the newspapers about why."

"Your brother James — I get the impression that he and Tim weren't close."

"Oh, do you? No, I don't think that's quite true." She collected up plates and pottered around in the kitchen while she thought. When she came back she said: "They weren't close in temperament, of course. James is a much more conventional, buttoned-up character. Frankly he's never had an original thought in his life. But I think James always admired Tim — his originality, his fun, his openness. He was at Eton with him, which can't have been easy at times —"

"No, indeed."

"— but James was always loyal to him, defended him when he needed it. Elder brothers aren't always so supportive at public school. Have you read Trollope's *Autobiography?*"

"I have. Quite horrific."

"There was only a couple of years between James and Timothy, and they always talked to each other, got advice from each other. I would have said in that sense they were close."

"Though it was you that Tim loved."

She smiled gratefully.

"Yes, I suppose so. I was the one he gave most time to, took most trouble over. If I didn't grow up into the typical deb I have Tim to thank for that. Tim was somehow apart, the one person in our family I could look at and say without hesitation: he is a real person, he is not locked in by prejudices and conventions, he doesn't live by Daddy and Mummy's assumptions — or anybody else's assumptions — he lives life to the full, and in his own way. Maybe if I'd not had Tim as a brother I would never have married Ferdy. Daddy was not pleased at the thought of a slightly mad Central European Jew as a son-in-law I can tell you!"

"But you got your own way."

"I got pregnant!" She smiled at the memory, which was clearly not at all shameful or painful to her. "That was in 1960, before the legalisation of abortion. He had us down to the Registry Office in no time!"

There was one more thing I had to ask about.

"Do you have any memories of the day of the murder?"

She looked down. We were eating apple pie by now, but I realized she had eaten very little of the meal she had cooked. This was the difficult part for her, the actual murder. She spoke slowly, carefully, as if even now she had to exercise restraint, for fear of breaking down.

"Of the day of the murder, nothing. It happened in the evening, and I was at another of those damned Suez demonstrations. He . . . he wasn't discovered till the next morning. I've always had nightmares of him lying there, not quite dead. It was the cleaning woman discovered him, when she came in at nine." She pointed towards the door, and I could see that her hand was shaking. "He was lying over there. He'd been horribly battered, then finished off by one terrible blow to the back of the head. Things were smashed all around him, the phone was off the hook, there was blood on the floor."

She put her face in her hands and closed her eyes.

"Don't go on if it's too painful."

"No, no, I'm all right. . . . That's my memory of it. I never saw him, of course — James identified the body, and I didn't come here for weeks afterwards. Then, when it was in the hands of agents who were letting it for me, I forced myself to come. Everything spoke of him — was horrible — and I was just letting myself out when I looked down, and over the stained floorboards there was a patch of brown — the blood the cleaner had been unable to get out. It was years before I could come back here. . . ." She swallowed and shook her head sadly. "And now I live here, cool as you like, and all my friends say, 'Belgravia — how grand!' and days and weeks go by without my thinking of him."

"Time heals."

"Time deadens, anyway . . . And yet always in the back of my mind there is that insistent feeling of betrayal, of my having failed him. And above all that sense of waste. I don't know what Tim would have done with his life, but I do know one thing: he would not have been negligible."

I nodded agreement. And I was suddenly seized with the notion that, ex-cabinet minister as I was, with — as the commentators say — solid achievements to my credit, I was somebody who had wasted his life. Marjorie had hit on the word. I was negligible.

7

A VIOLENT REACTION

I realize that even now I know nothing about Timothy's murder.

Oh, I know he was battered to death, presumably by Andrew Forbes, but that's about it. I could, perhaps, have pressed Marjorie Knopfmeyer, but her distress was so evident, still, after thirty-four years, that I shied away from the subject. In any case I doubt that she had much more to tell. Timothy's murder had fallen on her as such a sudden and a stunning blow that I had the impression that at the time she had shut her mind to the details. The *fact* of the death was so terrible that she had not wanted to know too much about the manner of it.

One of the advantages of having been a minister in several departments of government is that you have contacts — and often contacts who owe you favours — in all walks of life. Anyone who has been at the Home Office will have contacts with the police. As a matter of fact, since in my time there I had a fair amount to do with Northern Ireland I have still what might be described as a light police guard. Unfortunately the policeman who generally represents this vague official concern for my well-being is a torpid young man, and I could not imagine his being of any use to me in the Wycliffe matter (I can't imagine his being any protection against an IRA attack either, come to that). After my forced retirement I used him once or twice as a driver, but his conversation was so insipid and inhibited that even this perk was one I found I preferred to give up. Now we do no more than greet each other.

In my mind I went through the various police officers I know, and eventually I rejected all the serving officers in favour of a retired one. It was a matter of their likely reaction: serving officers can often regard requests from politicians as political pressurising, and they may react either in a hostile manner or a fawning one. With a retired officer I would have something in common. I had always got on well with Superintendent Sutcliffe, and though he has been retired now for two or three years, I guessed that he still had good contacts at Scotland Yard. What was more, I had his home address.

"Mr. Proctor, this is a surprise."

He had answered the phone after it had rung several times. He is a long, lean man with a tired moustache and something of the beagle in his expression. I pictured him as having come to the phone from trimming and tidying in his garden. I also pictured him as asking himself what on earth I could want from him, and he confirmed this by adding: "You do know I'm retired?"

"You and me both," I said. "If you call it retirement when you get the push."

"I did hear you were offered Northern Ireland," said Sutcliffe, with a trace of a chuckle in his voice.

"Being offered the Northern Ireland Secretaryship is like being told to dig your grave before you are shot," I said. "Metaphorically speaking, of course. Anyway, for my sins I'm writing my memoirs."

"Ah — politicians always do seem to, these days. I suppose we have Churchill to blame for that."

"No, it goes further back than that. Asquith and Lloyd George both wrote theirs. Politicians in general have an affinity for fiction. Anyway policemen seem to do pretty well by their memoirs these days. Aren't you going to cash in too?"

"Not me, sir. Policemen shouldn't write autobiographies. They play up their involvement with the sensational cases, hoping the newspapers will buy the serial rights."

"Politicians claim to have drafted all the popular legislation," I admitted, "and never have had anything to do with things like the poll tax or water privatisation. But anyway, the thing is, I've got sidetracked by something in your line."

"Oh?"

"By a friend who was murdered in his flat just off Belgrave Square in 1956."

"In 1956 I was a uniformed constable on the beat. And my beat certainly wasn't Belgrave Square."

"I never imagined that it was. The fact is, I want to find out as much as possible about the murder."

"Why?"

"Difficult to explain. I think it's a sort of guilt that it made so little impact on me at the time."

"I can understand that, sir. I've had colleagues who were killed in the line of duty, and it's always irked me that there's never been time for more than a tear or two and a shake of the head before we've had to get down to the next case. You're not thinking of one of those 'miscarriage of justice' books, are you, sir? I'd never have imagined that was your line of country."

"No, no. There was no miscarriage of justice. The boy fled the country and was never tried for the killing. It's not a question of who so much as of how and why. Timothy Wycliffe was such an engaging person, so popular and inoffensive, that I want to know how he came to be killed."

"Wycliffe . . . Would that be the political family, Mr. Proctor?"

"That's right. His father was Minister of Planning and Public Works at the time."

"One of your mob, sir. Some of your contacts in the party would know the details, wouldn't they?"

"They are clamping down. There are elements of scandal. Timothy was in the F.O. at the time, and a practising homosexual."

There was a chuckle from the other end of the line.

"Terribly afraid of scandal, politicians, aren't they, sir? It makes you wonder sometimes how they get up the courage to do the things they do. Well, I'll try to be of help. What exactly is it you want me to find out?"

"Quite simply I'd be interested in any information you can dredge up: who the murderer was, how they fixed on him, whether they were sure that it *was* him, any details of interest."

"Did the chap who did it flee the country

immediately, or did they have a chance to interview him?"

I thought.

"I'm not sure. I suspect immediately."

"That would be a pity . . . still, I'll see what I can get hold of."

"You still have contacts?"

"Of course. An ex-copper always has ways of finding things out."

"Really? An ex-politician is as dead as a doornail." I said this entirely without bitterness. I was beginning to find there was life, and a thoroughly good life, after politics. "Will you drop round and see me when you've got something? We could have a drink and go through it."

"I'll get on to you in a day or two's time, sir."

When I had put the phone down I sat thinking for a while. I was going back over that one memory I had had while talking to Marjorie Knopfmeyer, the memory I had not wanted to share with her. I tried to date it: it was not in the lead-up to the murder, because it was something that happened while I was still at the Foreign Office. I rather thought we were agonising at the time about our relationship with Europe — talking about how we couldn't go in with them because of our Special Relationship with the U.S., our

Commonwealth ties, and all that, rather like the woman who doesn't want to have too much to do with her next-door neighbours in case they get too pushy. Still, that doesn't exactly date it. I think it must have been round about 1953, by which time Tim and I were good friends and shared confidences quite naturally.

The memory starts with my coming upon Tim in the corridor. When I saw his face I said, "My God!"

"Had an argument with a revolving door," he said breezily.

"It obviously fought back."

He was lying, of course. The left side of his face was not only bruised, it had small cuts as well — the skin was livid, and the eye was swollen. I wouldn't have made the joke if there had been anyone else in the corridor, because we both recognised that within the context of the Foreign Office Tim had to lie. Whatever confidences he might make to me, officially a front had to be kept up. Of course Tim could have invented something better: a fight in which he had intervened to protect a young lady — something of that kind. But it was typical of Tim that he should come up with a *minimal* lie — a standard gesture, a tiny bob towards the official front.

We went about our business, but I had detected behind the breeziness an edge of worry or unhappiness. No one said anything much beyond the odd "Tim's been in the wars." Those, I suppose, were the outsiders' bobs towards the official front. But I am still not sure, in fact, just how much the average diplomat or civil servant in the F.O. knew at the time about Tim and his activities.

We finished late, and almost without needing to arrange it we went for a drink after work. The Waggon and Horses, near the St. James's Park tube station, was a quiet pub except at lunchtimes and at five o'clock. We got a corner to ourselves where we could talk, and I bought the first round. I noticed that Tim, unusually, asked for a double Scotch.

"All right, tell me about it," I said when we were settled. Tim smiled wryly.

"I got into a fight."

"I *know* you got into a fight, you ass. I gave up believing in aggressive revolving doors years ago. What kind of a fight? Not an after-hours brawl in the Old Kent Road, I take it?"

"A purely private brawl."

"You and him, behind closed doors?"

"Yes."

"Well, that's a blessing. A fight between consenting adults in private. No witnesses. You should have taken a couple of days off

105

work with a cold."

"This bruise isn't going to go away in a couple of days."

"Come on, how did it happen? I just can't imagine you getting into a fight."

"I don't know how it happened. . . . Funnily enough, I really *don't know*. You've got to believe that I'm not one of those people who get their kicks from violence. There are those who do, but I'm not one of them."

"I never thought you were. But you do go with rough trade."

How worldly wise I had become! The phrase just rolled off my tongue. Tim grimaced with distaste, then flinched in pain.

"I don't like the phrase."

"But it *is* trade, isn't it? You pay them."

"Sometimes."

"They're working-class boys who do it for money."

"*Yes*, most of them. Don't go all Mrs. Grundy on me."

"And you take them to your flat."

"Well, it's a lot more comfortable than a quick go in the park. Yes, they usually come to my flat."

"Is that wise?"

"Why not? Do you mean they might steal things from me?"

"Well, there is that, but it wasn't what I

was thinking about. Don't you think they might be struck by the contrast? Between your life and theirs?"

He sat for a moment looking into his glass.

"Do you think it could be that? I'd never thought of it. It's not as though it's an enormous flat, or a luxurious one. I don't set any great store by money — or comfort or possessions, come to that."

"That's all very fine when you have them," I said tartly.

He laughed, with a touch of his usual self.

"All right, that sounded pretty self-righteous. But give me a break, Peter. You can't say I've ever flaunted what I have."

"I didn't say you had. You don't have to flaunt them for the boys to be conscious that they're there, and to contrast them with the homes they come from, or the bed-sitters they live in. Don't you think they might be resentful that they're selling the most basic thing, their body, to someone who has so much?"

"Christ, you make me feel awful," Tim said, and went to the bar to get a second round.

"All right," I said when he came back. "Tell me what happened last night."

"Well, it was my birthday yesterday — I'm Virgo, believe it or not — and I picked up this boy in Trafalgar Square: nice lad, from

Glasgow — could hardly understand a word he said."

"And you went back to your flat?"

"That's right. We made love, I threw together a meal, we watched television —"

"Good God! I didn't know you'd bought a television set."

"The boys often like it. This Gavin did. He'd only seen it two or three times in his life before."

"Well, that's certainly the first time I've heard *that* given as a reason for buying television!"

"You are a frightful snob, Peter. You should get a set yourself. The programmes may be awful, but it's going to revolutionise the way people regard politicians. Anyway, we made love again, had a drink, and he got ready to go."

"Was there any . . . pent-up violence about this chap?"

"*No.* He was just very quiet."

"Had he anywhere to go?"

"Yes. Otherwise I'd have asked him to stay the night. He was down in London on a visit to an aunt in Islington."

"Then what happened?"

"I'd paid him — well. We were going towards the door and — I really don't remember in detail, but I think I put my arm around him and was going to kiss him goodbye when he shouted 'Keep your fuckin' hands to yourself' and pushed me, then punched me hard, then again, and I knocked my head against the side of the cabinet — very painful — and as I was reeling he kicked me in the groin and rushed out of the door."

"And you say he hadn't got any pent-up violence in him!"

"He *hadn't*, not before."

I thought for a long time before I said: "You must have got him to do things he didn't like doing."

"Then he made a bloody good pretence of liking them."

"People do, Tim. Look, it's got to be one of three things, hasn't it? Either he was doing things with you that he really found unnatural and disgusting, or he felt inferior, condescended to, and patronised —"

"I do not patronise or condescend to them!"

"But maybe your whole way of life makes them feel condescended to. Or thirdly he was just one hell of a violent young man. Glasgow's no town for softies."

"You can be tough without going in for unprovoked violence."

"You *can* be. But some tough people are just on the look-out for an excuse for a punchup."

Tim sat meditatively over his second large whiskey.

"It's upsetting . . . unnerving. I know these boys. . . . I thought I knew them."

"You don't get to know people on one-night stands."

At this time I had a flat in Victoria, and I remember thinking as I walked home how the basis of our relationship had changed. I still immensely admired Tim's political insight, his social savoir faire, his irrepressible gaiety, but I felt his superior in that worldly wisdom which comes from dealing in depth with people. There was, it seemed to me then, a naiveté about his view of others — maybe because of his fleeting sexual encounters, maybe because he had never had the experience of a close family life, maybe because of a temperamental inclination to see only the best in people. There was, still, something of the innocent about him. I didn't then wonder whether it would be the downfall of him, but I do wonder now if it was.

Looking back I see that, in those reflections, I was being very smug and self-congratulatory. My knowledge of people was not so much deeper than Tim's, my knowledge of myself much less. But remembering that incident does convince me of one thing: that a taste for violence was never part of Tim's sexual nature. Far from getting any masochistic pleasure from the incident, Tim reacted with bewilderment, pain, shock. He didn't understand how someone could behave in that way to him — someone to whom he had shown only friendship. I know people can develop tastes, sexual as well as any other sort, but I would be very surprised if Tim developed a liking for being on the receiving end of violence. I do not believe, then, that his death could have been the culmination of a beating-up of which he had at least begun as the willing victim.

I do think, though, that one of the three possibilities that I put to him at the time for the Scottish boy's violence may provide the explanation for what happened to him that night in 1956.

8

PORTRAIT of a KILLER?

Yesterday Sutcliffe rang me to tell me that he'd got hold of the basic facts of the case. He said he was free in the evening — in fact he said he was free every evening — so we arranged that he should come round here about half past six. When Nina showed him in (Nina is one half of the Filipino couple who live in the basement and cook and clean for us) I felt a lift when I saw his amiable and doggy form again — a lift, and also a spurt of fellow feeling: he had about him that indefinable something that said "retired." The feeling I had was the fellowship of the discarded: he and I were both rummaging on the rubbish-tip of life. He, pretty clearly, was enjoying it less than I.

"What will you have?" I asked. "There needn't be any nonsense about not drinking on duty now."

"That's very kind of you, sir. I'm really a draught bitter man —"

"I can manage an Australian beer."

"Don't make me laugh. I'll have a Scotch and water, sir, if you don't mind."

"Couldn't we get on Christian name terms? I'm Peter, as you know."

Sutcliffe shuffled his feet and looked a mite awkward.

"It doesn't slip easily off my tongue — I'm too wary of politicians — but I'll try. I'm John, though mostly in the force I was known as Sutty."

"That sounds too much like burning Indian widows. I'll stick with John." I came over with the drinks. "How does retirement suit you?"

"It'll be all right when I can stop my mind from being active," Sutcliffe said dourly. "And when I can get people out of the feeling that suddenly I need cossetting or 'brightening up.' And when I can stop my daughters bringing me round things in casseroles that 'only need heating up.' "

"Bad as that?"

He gave a slow grin.

"Not really. I'm leaving out the things that I'm glad to have got away from. Still, I've enjoyed looking into this."

He tapped his notebook, and I gestured towards the armchairs so we could go through it in comfort.

"I didn't push my luck by asking for photocopies," Sutcliffe said as a preliminary, "so I made a lot of notes, and the rest is in my head. Where shall we start?"

"Where the police came into it, I suppose," I said. "With the finding of the body."

"Right. That's perfectly straightforward. The cleaner came in on the Friday morning at ten past nine. She had her own key, of course, saw the body immediately and phoned the police. The phone was off the hook, but that was about the only thing she disturbed. She seems to have been a sensible body."

"What state was the flat in?"

"As you'd expect if there had been a rough-house: chairs overturned, furniture displaced, a vase and a chair broken. It didn't look, though, as if there'd been any deliberate orgy of destruction."

"Ah — I wondered. The boy seems to have been quite an ordinary lad, and a flat like that —"

"Right. What you might call a social re-sentment. It was something that occurred to me, and to the police at the time, but in fact most of the disorder and destruction seems to have been incidental to the fight."

"What about the violence to the body?"

"That was very considerable — bruises all over: to the face, legs, groin, and so on. There was a bad cut on the side of the face that had bled a lot before death. There were no abrasions or other damage to the knuckles, suggesting that he didn't actually counter the violence, merely tried to restrain his attacker. Does that surprise you?"

"No, it doesn't. He'd been attacked by a casual pickup once before, and he was very upset — hurt, if that's not a silly word. It would be very much in character for him to try to restrain rather than hit back."

"That was the picture the police had of the fight. At some point he got to the phone, presumably to call the police, but he was stopped — no 999 call was received from him. Eventually, the police hypothesize, he was simply knocked out."

"And then murdered?"

"Yes — a brutal blow on the back of the head, as he lay there. Some time later, the doctor thought — though like all such gentry he wasn't prepared to commit himself."

"I see . . . As if the boy thought about what he'd done, the seriousness of the assault, then decided he'd be safer if he actually finished him off?"

"Yes, something of that sort, the police thought. His fingerprints were all over the flat, by the way, but he didn't have any police record, so he probably banked on that saving him. . . . I don't imagine he was thinking very straight."

"Probably not." I sat thinking about the scene for some time, the last hour of Timothy Wycliffe. It was an ugly picture. "How did the police get on to him, this Andrew Forbes?"

"Ah, that's quite interesting. It wasn't for some time, and when they did they found that he'd already left the country."

"No interview with him then? That's a pity."

"It is. The fact is, they relied for their information about Mr. Wycliffe's habits and friends on his neighbours."

"The Belgrave Square mafia?"

"That's right — that's the impression the interview reports gave me: a really tight-knit community. There was a desire to hush up warring with a desire to gossip. If the police had had better links with homosexual circles they might have got to Forbes quicker, but for obvious reasons they didn't. And in fact it doesn't seem that Forbes was Wycliffe's principal boyfriend at the time of the murder."

"No?"

"Not according to the Belgrave Square residents. There was a great wad of interview reports in the records, and Forbes's name was never mentioned once."

"Whose names were?"

"Well, there were two men who had been at the flat — staying there — for longish periods over the summer and autumn of that year. One was called Gerald Fraser-Hymes, and the other Lawrence Cornwallis. I have addresses for them at the time of the investigation, though I don't imagine there'll be a great deal of joy there. They were both in flat or bed-sitter territory, with a transient population."

"The name of Lawrence Cornwallis seems to ring a vague bell," I said, trying to make concrete vague memories of reports read rather than people met. Nothing definite came. "I suppose these two were, to put it frankly, the sort of young men whom people in Belgravia might *know*. Their mob."

"That's my impression. Or, more distantly, that someone had known someone who'd known the mother — that sort of thing, and then the names and details had gone the rounds of the Square."

I remembered the unblushing snobbery of Lady Charlotte Wray and smiled.

"That figures. Name, school, family tree — 'I knew his poor grandmother' — that sort of thing. That's how the Square was at that time."

"No doubt there was a lot of that. Anyway, having those two names kept the police busy for a day or two, before they realized they had to look further."

"The two had alibis?"

"No — at least, not very convincing ones. The fact was, it wasn't either of their finger-prints all over the flat."

"But surely they could have worn gloves, and the Forbes prints remain from an earlier visit?"

He gave me the sort of pitying look that I probably give to people who show their ignorance of procedure in the House.

"You're talking like an amateur, Mr. Proctor . . . Peter. There are fingerprints and fingerprints. You don't hold a glass in the same way as you hold a crowbar. The police were pretty sure that the Forbes prints — as they turned out to be — were made in the course of the fight. Some were even bloody."

"I see. Yes, I can imagine you'd make a different sort of print, in different places than usual, in the course of a fight. At what stage, by the way, did the police realize that Tim was a practising homosexual?"

"The moment they began talking to people in the Square."

"Of course. Silly question."

"They may even have had their eye on him earlier — I got a hint or two of that from the records. Remember when this was. In the early fifties there'd been a number of what you might call 'show trials': an actor, a peer, and so on."

"I remember. To encourage the others. The son of a government minister might have been a suitable follow-up. That was something I was always trying to impress on Tim at the time. He was convinced the police used their own men in plain clothes as bait."

"They did. I'm not defending or apologising, just stating: they did."

"You weren't yourself involved?" I asked mischievously.

"Not attractive enough by half!" Sutcliffe grinned as he got a mental picture of his youthful self. "And by the way it was the sort of job you could refuse, and I would have. Quite a lot rather enjoyed it."

"Which says something about them."

"Right. Well that's enough breast-beating. Let's get back to Andrew Forbes. The police didn't get hold of the name from the Belgrave Square mob, though later several confirmed that they'd seen a chap like that visiting the flat from time to time. As you say, Forbes wasn't the sort whose mummy they knew back in the twenties. His name came from Fraser-Hymes, one of the two friends. No doubt both men were feeling pretty hard-pressed, and with reason, and Fraser-Hymes named names. In fact there was a whole list of people whom the police contacted and took prints and statements from."

"Which led eventually to Andrew Forbes?"

"Or rather to his flat. By then the bird had flown: he'd taken the night ferry to Dieppe on the second of November, the night after the murder. His landlady let our chaps into his flat, and there they found prints everywhere which matched the ones from Craven Court Mews."

"Had Forbes given up his flat?"

"No, he hadn't. He'd just said to his landlady that he'd be away for a few nights. He'd taken a case full of clothes, toilet things, and that's about all."

"Did the police get to know much about him? All that I know is that he was an unemployed electrician."

"Even that's misleading — technically true, but misleading. Makes him sound like a down-and-out or a male prostitute who couldn't give his real job. It wasn't like that at all. Forbes had had a good job with the BBC for two and a half years. Commercial television had started up the previous year, and he had a job lined up with them, at better pay. When the BBC heard this they sacked him. They were very snooty about ITV in those days.

So Forbes had money in the bank, a small but nice flat, good prospects."

"Not quite the picture I had of him."

"No. Background: respectable working class in Nottingham. I've got the address of his parents — here, I'll leave it with you, though I doubt it will be of much use. Curriculum vitae: good reports from his Secondary Modern school, though he certainly wasn't the academic type; apprenticeship at fifteen, job at the end of it, then moved to London and the job at the BBC in 1954."

"Did the landlady know him at all?"

"Oh yes — she lived on the ground floor, and Forbes had the flat at the top. Chatted to him a lot, gave him cups of tea. Liked him very much, said he was quiet, kept the flat clean, never any trouble beyond once or twice returning home drunk."

"Boyfriends?"

"No. In fact she was convinced he had a girlfriend. But you've got to remember, Peter, when we are talking about. As far as the landlady was concerned they would be *friends*, not boyfriends. 'Coming out' at that date could have meant being put inside. The landlady said he had a few friends, chaps of his own kind from work, and some of them she recognised, but no one specially close, she said. He kept in touch with his family, rang them once a week, went home for holidays and the odd weekend. Liked pop music and football, supported Arsenal, went to the occasional dance. And that was about it: the typical young man of the fifties."

"That's the picture of an unlikely murderer. Did that strike the police too?"

A slightly cynical smile wafted across Sutcliffe's lips.

"Are you *sure* you're not on to one of these 'miscarriage of justice' kicks, sir?"

"Not at all — I'm just interested in the pressures that made this particular young man into a murderer."

"As far as that goes you could say that to the police there is no such thing as an unlikely murderer: depends on the person, depends on the pressures. I think the police at that time took it as some kind of lovers' tiff."

"Some tiff."

"Quarrel. Again, remember the times: there was a tendency among the investigating policemen to regard homosexuals as by definition excitable and unstable."

I followed this up.

"Then again, a *lovers'* tiff. I can't see that it was established that they were particularly close."

Sutcliffe nodded.

"Certainly the impression I got was that the

other two men were much closer to him: both of them had spent periods of ten days or more in the flat in the months before the murder. So far as I can tell from the notes, Andy Forbes seems to have been more in the nature of an occasional lay — ugly word, sorry."

"What about his family?"

"Denied indignantly that he was a homosexual. What you'd expect, really. Probably that was the reason he came to London. They certainly weren't able to point to any regular girlfriend while he lived in Nottingham, or anyone he'd brought home since. Remember that the working-class reaction to homosexuality is a gut one: they are less liberal than the middle class even, and certainly less so than the upper classes."

I thought hard for a while.

"Right, well I think I've got a much better picture of the murder. What about afterwards? Did the police get any further leads on Andrew Forbes?"

"Leads? I don't know if you'd call them that. Rumours, really. The sort of thing you get in all missing-and-wanted cases. Is there anywhere in the world, I wonder, where Lord Lucan hasn't been spotted? The best authenticated were that he was working as a barman in Las Palmas in the spring of 1957, and as an electrician in Barcelona in 1958. Remember this was at the height of the Franco era."

"I know: no extradition."

"That's right. And a police force better at intimidation than investigation. There was a request to the Barcelona police to investigate the last report, but by the time they got around to it he had got hold of a false passport and flown."

"Where to?"

"America, they thought."

"The States? Canada? Dear old South America, haven for all the world's undesirables, and fit punishment for them too, from all I've heard?"

"The word from the Barcelona police was that it was the States. I don't know how much trust I'd put in that."

"And there the trail ends, I suppose."

"Pretty much so. I gather from the case notes, though, that there was a reporter interested at the time."

That made me sit up.

"Really? That does surprise me. The lady who does research for the memoirs hasn't turned up anything of substance from the newspapers yet."

"I don't suppose she will. Terry Pardick was a crime reporter for the *Daily Mail*. What they'd have done if it had been a child of one of the Labour Party notables, say Hugh

Gaitskell or Jim Callaghan, I don't know, but as it was the son of a Tory cabinet minister they weren't interested unless it was absolutely hard."

"So presumably he never got that far?"

"Presumably not. I knew him some years later. He was a nasty little muckraker, was Terry Pardick — a terrier with a nose for rotting meat."

"I don't recall having heard the name. He was no Chapman Pincher, obviously."

"Definitely not, if only because he couldn't distinguish the truth from rumour."

"A *Private Eye* man before his time."

"Something of the sort. He may well have got no further than the fact that Timothy Wycliffe was a homosexual. Certainly the *Mail* didn't print that, or anything else. Whether he got anything into any other rag I don't know — even then there were rags that would print any dirt provided it was dirt. All the police knew was that he was following them around, getting on to the ring of his boyfriends and so on."

"I'll tell Elspeth Honeybourne to look at the seamy end of Fleet Street, but I rather imagine she's doing that anyway. This Pardick is dead, is he?"

Sutcliffe pulled at his ear, and looked very like a beagle who has been distracted from an interesting scent.

"I'm assuming so. I haven't heard his name for years."

"I made that assumption about Tim's father, but I was wrong. Look, John, I'm very grateful. All this has really put me in the picture. I don't like to ask this, but are you willing to do a little more?"

Sutcliffe smiled.

"I thought you'd never ask. Yes, I am. A little light work — isn't that what the experts always recommend for us superannuated professionals?"

I thought hard.

"Now, I'm off to Derbyshire next Monday. I could well take in Nottingham on the way back. Not that I expect any joy there. Even if I traced any member of his family, it's not likely that they'd know anything."

"I'm not so sure, sir . . . Peter. He could have contacted them again. He could do that easily enough without our knowing. In fact, he could have been in contact with them the whole time."

"It's a thought."

"You've got their old address there. It's a start."

His optimism perked me up. Of course if they were a close family Andy Forbes would have tried to keep in touch. Not that what he told them was necessarily reliable.

"Then there are the two friends. I could put Elspeth on to them. . . . Why does that name Lawrence Cornwallis ring a bell?"

"I couldn't say, Mr. Proctor, because it doesn't."

"It has a ring of the Great and Good — the sort of person who sits on a Royal Commission, is a governor of the BBC or *The Observer*, gets interviewed on radio about homelessness or pornography. . . . Not in politics, of course, or I'd know him. . . . Could it be in the literary world. Or the church?"

"Shouldn't be difficult to trace, if that's the case."

"True. Now, I was wondering if you could get on to Terry Pardick. You must have contacts in Fleet Street."

"Oh yes, I have a few still. I suppose the main thing is to find out if he's still alive?"

"And if he's not, if anyone was working with him on the Wycliffe case at the time. He may have had some sort of junior or cub reporter with him. . . . That's all that springs to mind at the moment. Can you think of anything else?"

Sutcliffe flicked through his notebook and then stood up.

"I think I've told you everything of any importance. Oh, but there was one detail, though, in all the stuff about the Belgrave Square residents, and the account they gave of Mr. Wycliffe and his friends."

"Yes?"

"When they interviewed a Lady Charlotte Wray, one of the names she mentioned was yours."

9

STRATEGIES

"I heard you and that policeman when I came in," said Jeremy over dinner, with a mildly derisive smile on his face. "You sounded like a couple of schoolboys."

"Nonsense — we were planning strategies. But he did tell me something rather ironic: in the original investigation of Tim's death my name came up."

"*Really?* Reminder of your gay youth?"

"Not at all," I said with dignity. "Merely a nasty-minded and stupid old lady enjoying her moment in the limelight by naming any and every young man she could think of. Still, it was pretty funny after all this time, and made me feel I'd come full circle by going into Tim's death as I am."

"So how come Special Branch at the time didn't come round demanding to see your sexual credentials?"

"I should think I was pretty far down on the list, and long before they would have got to me they found their man."

"I thought they never did find their man?"

"They never *got* him. He'd done a flit to Spain."

"You think they got it right?"

"I suppose so. But from everything we've dug up so far he seems to have been such an ordinary working-class chap . . . I imagine they were very relieved that he was, so to speak, such a long way from Belgravia. Sighs of relief all round. In the fifties Belgravia spelt influence as well as money."

"Didn't it always?"

"You'd have thought so, but I don't think it always did. I'm reading *Philip* at the moment —"

"So I noticed. Why *Philip* of all novels?"

Jeremy did a degree in English literature, but he's in the City at the moment. He reads painfully little.

"Some hope of finding an undiscovered masterpiece, I suppose," I said. "The childish hope that the ugly duckling will turn out to be a swan."

"And is it?"

"Absolutely not. I've never known anyone tell an all right story in a more infuriatingly desultory way. I think Thackeray started going senile the moment he'd finished *Vanity Fair*. Anyway, at one point somebody is ad-

130

vised to stop living above their means and take a house in 'a quiet little street in Belgravia somewhere — nobody will think a penny the worse of you.' That rather puts Belgravia in its place."

"Was it Belgravia put the police on to this chap?"

"No, though doubtless it would have if it had 'known' him. Unfortunately their view was restricted to their own little circle. But I bet they were quietly cock-a-hoop when the police decided it was him."

Jeremy nodded. I think he's beginning to get interested.

"What next then, Dad?"

"I don't know. . . . Andrew Forbes seems to have landed up in the States. I think I'll give Reggie a ring."

"He'll start pressing you to go out on a visit, and then you'll start getting all broody about seeing your grandson."

"I *am* broody about seeing my grandson." My only grandson was born in America, and has not been brought over for my inspection. I do very much look forward to seeing him. "I'd like to make sure he isn't being choked by the smog of Los Angeles, or turning into a gum-chewing, wise-cracking little smart alec."

"How old is he now? Eighteen months?"

"They grow up early there."

Jeremy had a point, of course. I suppose I was feeling a bit dynastic, and wishing that the son and heir of my son and heir could grow up in this country. All rather silly. One thing I am quite sure of is that Downing Street is not going to offer me a hereditary peerage!

"You're very prejudiced," Jeremy said. "I've known lots of charming Americans."

"So have I," I agreed. "It's just that the charming ones are rarely the ones in politics, and it's people in politics I've mostly met."

"I don't think politicians in this country are long on charm either," said Jeremy meanly.

Perhaps that is one reason why I remain fascinated by Timothy's fate: he had a charm which I have seldom encountered in my daily life since. And that charm was so at odds with the manner of his death. Jeremy, in spite of his burgeoning interest, doesn't really understand why I should be so preoccupied with a straightforward murder (or manslaughter) case of thirty-odd years ago. When I sit down and think about it I am never altogether sure of my motives. For example, I sometimes think I might make a book out of it. It would be a damned sight more interesting than my memoirs. Then when I wonder whether Andrew Forbes was in fact Tim's killer I start wondering whether I'm *hoping* this, to make a more interesting book.

These days, you notice, I am a prey to self-doubt, as I seldom was when I was active in politics, and this may be the result of being sacked. On the other hand I do at times seem to be developing the blinkered vision that investigative journalists sometimes develop when on a story — the vision that enables them to see only those facts that fit in with their theory. When I try to analyse the fascination that the case has for me, two things predominate: the motivation for the crime, and the feeling that, for homosexuals, that was another world. Put your average young person back in 1956 and he would notice big differences, but he would soon acclimatise himself and feel at home. Put a young homosexual back then and for him it would be like going back to the Dark Ages.

Whether I could convey this if I did write a book about Timothy and his death I don't know. I am not an imaginative person.

Ringing my son in Los Angeles is a bit of a problem. He is usually at home in the evenings since they had the child, but, the time difference being what it is, I am always in bed by then. I can ring him at the office, but then I at best catch him on the wing, shouting instructions about this and that and putting other calls on hold, so that it is impossible to have a meaningful conversation. On the whole it's best to do the mathematics (oh for the time when a civil servant would have done it for me!) and try to catch him at home in the morning, before he sets out through, and contributes to, the fog and pollution of the streets.

"Did I get the time right?" I asked when I got through.

"You sure did. It's a quarter to seven."

"Oh dear: I meant it to be a quarter to eight."

"Junior woke us anyway."

"Junior! How is . . . Howard?"

I find it difficult to say the name. Calling a baby Howard is not English, and it doesn't even abbreviate satisfactorily. I am inhibited from expressing any opinion, however, by the fact that Reggie complains bitterly about having been called Reginald. He says quite rightly that no one in Britain in the sixties was christened Reginald, that in the States it is an even more ludicrous name (he is known at the office as Richard), and that it made his schooldays a hell of ridicule. In fact, though I was very fond of Reggie Maudling, in retrospect he does not seem to have been a happy choice to name a baby after.

"He's fine. All the normal things are happening."

"Have you put his name down for a good psychiatrist yet?"

"Very funny, Pop. That's your jibe for the day. You don't have to underline what you think of America and the Americans. What did you actually ring me for?"

I had told him last time I had rung about my interest in Timothy Wycliffe's death. He had expressed benevolent approval, in the usual manner of the child who is glad his oldie has got something to occupy his time with. Wonderful how irritating one's own children can be! Now I filled him in briefly with some of the details I had learnt from Sutcliffe, and then came to the point.

"I wondered if you knew any private detectives."

"The firm uses them quite a lot."

Reggie is a statistician with a large insurance company. I'd thought that they probably would use private detectives to look into possibly fraudulent claims.

"Could you suss me out a good one?"

"Sure. And what you want is for him to get a lead on this Andrew Forbes?"

"That's the idea."

"What have you got on him so far?"

"Well, nothing much beyond the fact that he entered the States, presumably illegally, around 1958."

There were a few moments' silence at the other end.

"I'm definitely beginning to think you've gone a bit odd in your retirement, Pop."

I felt rebuked.

"Oh, and he'd probably be working in radio or television, or in the electrical industry somewhere."

"Have you any idea how many radio and television stations there are in this country? Have you any idea how many different industries employ electricians? You've got to give the man something, for Christ's sake."

"I used to go to my civil servants with a question and they'd come up with an answer. I didn't have to tell them what the answer was first."

"I bet you did. And I bet the answer they came up with was a plausible lie that you could get away with in the Commons. Probably some fiddled statistic."

My son feels strongly about the misuse of statistics, though I tell him that a statistical lie is morally no worse than all the other sorts of lie that politicians of all parties tell from time to time.

"Well," I said, a little shamefacedly, "what is the sort of information you think I should try to come up with?"

"A place where he might have settled, the

branch of electrical work he might have gone into, some idea of the sort of direction he might have gone in when choosing his name, that sort of thing."

"Really, one might as well forget the private detective if I'm to do most of his work for him," I grumbled. "But I'll see what I can do. Love to Helen. Give . . . Howard a hug from me."

"When are you coming out to see him?"

"You never know. It might be sooner than you expect, if the private eye comes up with anything."

I put down the phone and tried to settle to a little work on the memoirs, always with the problem of how to get a lead on Andrew Forbes jigging around in the back of my mind. Though the writing of the book is becoming much easier, it is really rather boring, and if it is boring to me, the subject, how much more boring is it likely to be to the reader? I feel it is fortunate that it already has a publisher, and one who has paid me an advance, otherwise it might land up as an unpublished manuscript in the archives of Conservative Central Office. Finally I called it a day, took up the slip on which Sutcliffe had written Andrew Forbes' home address in the fifties, and dialled Directory Enquiries.

"What town?"

"Nottingham."

"What name?"

"It's not a name, it's an address: 35 Exhibition Road."

"Sorry, we have to have a name."

"Try Forbes."

Almost immediately, such are the marvels of modern technology, the answer came back: "Sorry, no Forbes at that address."

So, no joy. Hardly surprising. Still, I decided to put that and the problem of the two friends to Elspeth Honeybourne, who was due in the morning. However, to forestall one of her well-concealed glances of pity at my incompetence I took the precaution of getting down *Who's Who*. There was no entry for Gerald Fraser-Hymes, but under Lawrence Cornwallis I struck lucky:

Cornwallis, Lawrence Edward: b. 20 June 1930; Educ. Harrow; Magdalene College Cambridge; Slough Theological College. Curate of St. Mary's, Kingston-upon-Hull . . .

And so on through various pastoral appointments and better until his (presumably) present post: "1985 Archbishop of Canterbury's special adviser on urban affairs, attached to Rochester Cathedral."

The entry went on to detail the various Royal Commissions he had sat on, the public enquiries and the prestigious appointments in the seventies that had left his name impressed on my mind as one of the Great and Good. He had been less active in recent years, of course, because the Prime Minister who was my boss did not love the Great and Good, and the feeling was returned. Anyway, there he was. He named his hobbies as opera and fell-climbing.

I was glad I'd thought to do this elementary piece of research, because Elspeth, when she came with a great bundle of stuff about my activities during the miners' strike and the great shutdown of '73-'74 (God how lacklustre my political career seems, when I have to go through it in detail!), was briskly dismissive about the other problems.

"We can try old telephone directories for the Forbes problem — if their son was only twenty-four in 1956 they probably lived for some time after that. Most people are on the telephone at some period of their lives, especially when they're getting old. Plenty of fallback possibilities if that doesn't work. Now, this other chap, Gerald Fraser-Hymes: you've no information of any sort about him? No school, career, parents? Nothing?"

"Nothing at all."

"Well, we'll try trade directories, school lists, and so on. Timothy Wycliffe's friends would generally have been of the old-school type, I suppose?"

"No — no, I really don't think that was the case. All across the board I'd have said."

"Well, with a name like Fraser-Hymes I don't think I'd try the Battersea Comprehensive first off. Leave it to me. I expect I'll come up with something."

Really she should have been a private detective. Though I suppose the things she works on are a lot more interesting than the things most private detectives work on.

She rang a few hours later with a number. She said that Forbes, F., had been listed at 35 Exhibition Road for nearly twenty-five years, from 1955 to 1979. Presumably he or she had either died or sold the house, but it could be they could no longer afford the expense of a telephone, and it could be that the present occupant, if it was not the parents themselves, would know something of the family. It seemed worth a try, Elspeth said, and I agreed.

I gave some thought to how to approach the tenant of 35 Exhibition Road, but I encountered the usual problems of area code changes and extra numbers to insert, so that by the time I got through I was flustered and merely improvising.

"Three-five-seven, six-one-four."

The voice was rich — a light contralto with more overtones of country than of city.

"Oh hello, I wonder if you could help me — it's Mrs. —?"

"Nicholls. Mavis Nicholls. And I should tell you that if you're selling double-glazing —"

"No, no. Nothing of that kind. I'm trying to trace a family that used to live at 35 Exhibition Road. That is your address, isn't it?"

"Ye-es."

"The family's name was Forbes . . ." There was no response from the other end, not even audible breathing, and I floundered on. "The initial was F. I wondered if you bought the house from them."

After a time I got a response.

"What exactly do you want to contact the family for, Mr., er . . . ?"

"Proctor. Peter Proctor. Well, it's in connection with a book I'm writing —"

"I can't see why anyone would write a book about our family. No call to do that."

"Ah — so you're a member of the family?"

There was a definite hesitation, then she said reluctantly: "Yes, I'm the daughter. Fred Forbes was my dad."

"And he's dead?"

"Died ten years ago — no, eleven. Mum

had gone the year before. I came in for the house, so we moved here."

"I'm sorry, Mrs. Nicholls. Now, the person I'm interested in wasn't your father, but your brother." I had put it too baldly. Again there was absolute silence. I added: "Your brother Andrew."

"I heard you. . . . Haven't I heard your voice before somewhere? And your name?"

"Maybe. I used to be in politics."

"I don't want anything to do with politicians! We've had enough trouble with them!"

"I'm sorry to hear that."

"If you know about Andy you should know that. Wasn't that Timothy Wycliffe a politician?"

"Well, no: he was a civil servant actually."

"Same thing as far as I can see. It's all the same mob. And I do know his father was a cabinet minister, because the police went on about it at the time."

"Yes, that is true. . . . Mrs. Nicholls, please believe that I don't mean your brother any harm —"

"There's no way you can harm him now. He's dead."

She said it rather quickly, as if she'd suddenly decided to say it. Wouldn't it have been more natural if she had told me that when his name first came up? I decided to reserve judgment as to whether or not it was true.

"Again, I'm sorry. But truly I mean no harm to his memory. The fact is, as I said, I'm a politician, or was, and I'm writing my memoirs. I've become fascinated by Timothy Wycliffe's death. He was a friend of mine, you see —"

"Oh yes?" Definite access of suspicion.

"Not in that way. More of a colleague. We worked together at the Foreign Office. I should tell you that the only person I've talked to who had met your brother liked him, and reports from his landlady and so on say what a pleasant young man he was."

If that sounds condescending, she didn't take it so.

"Well that's nothing but the truth. Everyone liked our Andy."

"So there's no question at all of my wanting to blacken his memory, or anything of that kind. I'm really interested in . . . well, how it happened. So I'd like to talk about him, what sort of a person he was, how he came to . . ."

I paused, not knowing how to put it, and she immediately broke in with "He didn't kill him!"

"I didn't say he did. We both know that it never came to a trial . . ."

"That's right. He's innocent until proved

143

guilty. That's British law, that is."

"That's right. But as I say, I'd like to talk to you about what you know —"

"I don't know much. Only what I heard. I was here in Nottingham at the time."

"All the same, I'd be interested to hear about your brother. As I'm going to be in the area next Monday I wondered if I could call on you."

She had obviously been expecting this, but still there was a long pause.

"Would that be evening? After dark?"

"Well, yes, it could be, if that suited you."

"I mean, you're known, aren't you?"

"Well, just a little. People sometimes recognise me in the street."

"No offence, it's just that the neighbours might see you and ask questions. We've had our fill of neighbours and their questions in our time, I can tell you!"

"Yes, I can imagine that. Well, could we say Monday at eight?"

There was another pause before she finally took the plunge.

"Yes. Yes, I suppose that'd be all right."

10

ANOTHER SISTER

The business that took me up to Derbyshire yesterday was connected with IMC, the computer firm of which I am a director. I took on a few directorships after I left government and parliament — just enough to ensure I could keep up the house in Barkiston Gardens and not so many as to interfere with work on the memoirs (this was when I was still hopeful of producing something somebody might want to read). My duties with the firm are largely ceremonial, and indeed it was merely a lunch I went up for — I represented the parent company. It was sufficiently tedious, but I had done my directorial duty by the late afternoon. I explored Derby, found it a handsome city, and then took the train to Nottingham as soon as the rush hour had died down.

I was still early for my appointment with Mrs. Nicholls. I checked into my hotel, had a quick shower, then took a taxi. The driver wanted to talk about football, and Nottingham Forest's fortunes. I made the sort of noises I used to make in Cabinet. I asked him to put me off at the end of Exhibition Road. Then I walked down it in the gathering gloom, going up little side streets, round blocks, soaking up the atmosphere and trying to get an idea of a childhood spent in this area. My own childhood had been spent among substantial detached houses in a tree-lined residential area — all rather stuffy and "let's keep ourselves to ourselves." The houses in Exhibition Road were Victorian terraced houses of red brick, solidly built, with two good-sized rooms and a kitchen on the ground floor (or so I imagined from what I could see), two bedrooms on the second, and a roomy attic, which most of the houses had converted into children's bedrooms, to judge by the modern dormer windows let into the roofs. There were many worse places to live — most modern semis for a start, not to mention the hideous modern estates put up by mass-market building firms. Here the walls would be thick, the ceilings high, the kitchen warm, and the center of family life. There were corner shops, a pub called the Duke of York, and the occasional family butcher, baker, and greengrocer, holding on still against the odds, like so many small businesses. There were no gardens to speak of, though, and only a rather scrubby patch of open land to play on. Houses such as those on Exhibition Road are beginning to seem desirable now — perhaps one more consequence of the Prince of Wales's evangelism. Forty years ago they would have been much less so: certainly this can never have been a prestige address.

By the time I went up to the door of number thirty-five there was little light left, and no neighbours at windows. Through the windows where the curtains were left undrawn I could see televisions on — "Coronation Street," probably, or the "Holiday Programme." The door was answered very quickly — doubtless Mavis Nicholls had been hovering in the hall.

"Oh, hello, Mr. . . . er, Proctor, wasn't it? Come in. Now I can see your face I do remember you from the television."

She was distinctly nervous, and talked about me as if I had been host on some discontinued game show. She knew my voice and my face, but my name meant nothing to her, and I was sure she could never have named any Cabinet post I had held. Sobering, that. Fame in the television age! She ushered me inside and into the front room, where a gas fire was burning and cups and plates of biscuits had been set out on the table.

"Would you like a cup of tea? I'm just making a pot. Or would you prefer coffee?"

"Tea would be fine."

She bustled off towards the kitchen, and I looked around. Elderly but comfortable furniture of the usual deplorable British design. All post-Andrew, no doubt. But a homely, lived-in room, which was not always true of "best" rooms.

"It's a nice house," I said, when Mrs. Nicholls came back.

"I like it. We had a semi in a nicer area, but when I came into this — when Dad died — we decided to move in here. It had memories, you see, and the three kids were still at home then, and they could have a bedroom each. Later on we were glad that's what we decided to do. Les — that's my husband — lost his job in 1982, and having this house without a mortgage on it was a godsend. I don't know how we'd have managed otherwise."

"He's got another one now?"

"Works as a barman in one of the pubs in the centre. He's a skilled engineer and it's not what he's used to, but it doesn't do to complain. There's many worse off."

"I've been walking around," I said, accepting a cup, "trying to imagine what a childhood was like in this street."

It sounds patronising now I put it down on paper, but she was not a prickly soul and she didn't take it as such.

"It was good — quite good really. It was my childhood here made me want to come back. There were lots of other children, of course, and we played in the streets because no one much around here had cars then — yes, it was all right. Warm and . . . nice. A good place to grow up."

"How many children were there in the family?"

"Just the two of us. Mum couldn't have any after me. Andy was the elder by two years. Money was always a bit short. Dad had come down from Derbyshire and he was unemployed for two years before Andy was born. But he always had work when I was growing up, and we never went hungry. If money was a bit tight the reason was that they were buying this house. Mum worked in shops, did some charring, anything going really, so a lot of my early memories of Andy are of him looking after me."

She sat down with her cup on the other side of the gas fire, and I was able to get a good look at her. She was a woman in her early fifties, inclining to plumpness. She had probably never been more than mildly pretty, but she had made the best of herself tonight

— had her hair done, put on a pretty frock — perhaps in anticipation of a visit from a "name." She gave the impression of someone who, now the children were grown up, had a lot of time on her hands, though she also seemed bright and resourceful, the sort who would always find useful ways of filling it. She was welcoming, fluent, in spite of a certain shyness. She was also tense and on her guard.

"I loved him," she said, unprompted. "I looked up to him and I loved him. He was so good to me, even though he was only the two years older: he took me to school, protected me from the bigger children, made me sandwiches if I was hungry. 'Let's do you up then, me duck,' he used to say, doing up the buttons on my coat, or tying my shoelaces. Things other boys around here would have been shy of doing for their kid sisters. When I got a bit older it was wartime, of course, and he'd make sure I could put my gas mask on, took me to the air-raid shelter, all that sort of thing."

"A considerate person."

"Yes — very. You probably think I'm whitewashing him. I'm not. There was a lot of mischief, a lot of ragging of teachers — there were some wartime replacement teachers who were not up to much. But Andy was never a worry to Mum or Dad. They knew he'd turn out all right. . . ."

I said diffidently: "That must have made it all the more . . . shocking when they found out."

She looked down into her lap, then nodded.

"Yes . . . He'd been gone to London then some years, of course. But he'd always come back at holiday times, and for weekends. He was getting on so well, earning good money . . ."

"You didn't know anything about his . . . private life."

Mrs. Nicholls looked up at me pleading, and a blush spread up from her neck and over her whole face. I realized with a stab of surprise that this, not the murder, was the thing she most dreaded talking about; that this was still to her something unmentionable, almost inconceivable.

"No . . . 'course we didn't. Dad and Mum would make remarks. When he came back for my wedding, 1955 that was, they'd say: 'Your turn next, Andy' and 'When are you going to bring a nice girl home, son?' And Andy would say: 'When I can find someone as nice as Mavis.' It was just a laugh. No one suspected . . . I mean, that just wasn't something anyone knew about round here."

"And it still bothers you?"

"Yes it does! I hate the very thought of it.

When Andy sent us the snaps of him and his first kiddy from San —"

She stopped and swallowed.

"Yes?"

"— from Santiago I thought 'Thank God!' and I was that pleased I was walking on air for a week."

At last — information. Children, presumably marriage, and a place to pin him to. Or was there?

"Santiago," I said. "That's in Chile. I didn't know he went to South America."

She was more visibly flustered than at any time in the interview.

"Oh no, I don't think that was South America. I think this was a place of the same name in America."

"The United States?"

"That's where Andy lived, the United States, right up to the time that he died."

"And that was —?"

"Two years ago. Nineteen eighty-eight. He wasn't old."

Mrs. Nicholls was showing signs not just of confusion but of distress — talking too quickly, flushing again. I noted it, to draw my own conclusions later on. I thought it would be politic to go back to the time of the murder.

"How did you get to hear about Andy's

. . . involvement in the Timothy Wycliffe murder?"

"Well, the police came round, of course. Les and I were living in a council flat then. Mum sent a neighbour's kid around, and when I got here — well, I can't describe it: it was as if her world had fallen apart. She couldn't stop crying. And Dad wouldn't believe it — not for days, not weeks. He went around saying: 'Nobody's going to tell me that our Andrew is a pansy.' "

"It was that that got to him?"

"Yes. I suppose you think that's foolish, you being more sophisticated and more used to that kind of thing. But it's the truth. It was that made him feel he couldn't hold up his head. Well, those weeks certainly sorted out who our friends were, I can tell you."

"I suppose so. There must have been a lot of talk."

"Well, talk you'd expect. There's always talk about a murder, and as to the other, people round here don't like that sort of thing, like I said. We're ordinary folk and we think it's just . . . disgusting. But the ones who were real friends came round — maybe just to have a kind word with Mum, maybe brought a cake — any little thing, just to show their sympathy. We didn't look for much, Mr. Proctor. As to the others — the rats I call them — well, I've never forgiven some of them for the things they said to Mum and Dad. Even today I can hardly be civil to them."

"When did you first hear from your brother?"

She bit her lip, uncertain how honest to be. She handed me the plate of biscuits, then went on, slowly, carefully.

"Well, it wasn't long after. Maybe three weeks. We got a note from Spain, sent under cover to Stan and Betty Martin down the road — they were Mum and Dad's best friends, and they were real bricks all through. The note just said not to believe what people were saying about him, and it gave a time and a date when he'd try to ring us, if we could be at the Martins'."

"And did he?"

"Oh yes. Andy was a real family boy: he knew how we'd be suffering. He wrote or rang regularly after that, usually through the Martins, because he didn't feel safe ringing here. It was years before he'd ring this house, scared the phone was being tapped. He always sent letters to the Martins until after our Janie was married. He'd taken a real shine to her when they'd met, and when she settled down he wrote to her. He still — right up to the time he died — sent his letters to her. He thought the police might intercept mail, and anything from America might be opened, especially with his . . . especially with his being on the run and all that."

She was getting confused again, repeating herself and suddenly changing what she had nearly fallen into saying. That, at any rate, was my impression, though I kept my face impassive, letting no shadow of suspicion show.

"What did he tell your dad and mum about that night?"

"Not much. He said there'd been a fight, and that this Wycliffe was alive when he left the flat. He didn't need to say more than that. Our Andy was always truthful, straight as they come, and he certainly wouldn't lie to Mum or Dad."

Except, perhaps, if he judged the truth too painful for them to bear.

"Did they ever go and see him?"

"No, they didn't. People like us didn't just hop on to planes in those days, did they? Mum was scared out of her wits by the very thought of flying. But I think they would have done eventually, because Andy was pressing them and saying he'd pay the fares. But then Mum contracted muscular dystrophy — oh, it must have been about 1968, and she was an invalid for the rest of her life. Dad retired early so he could nurse her."

"So you went instead."

I put it as a statement. She pursed her lips up, took my cup and poured me another cup of tea. She pressed more biscuits on me, as something to do, then sat down again. She was going to tell me something — how much, and how truthful it would be, I would have to judge when I could sit down and think it through.

"Yes, I did go. Me and Janie and Terry — my two eldest. Ellie, the youngest, has the same fear of flying that her grandma had, so she stayed at home with Les. . . . I'm not going to tell you much about the trip, and you can fish as much as you like, it won't make no difference. We all got on very well together. His two were much younger than my two, of course, but Janie mothered them. His wife was rather American, not what I was used to, but we hit it off really well. I got to like her. We did the usual things — went to Disneyland, and so on. I think Terry's still got his Disneyland T-shirt that Andy bought for him that time. It was a happy trip, one I'll never forget."

"And you talked about the night of the murder."

"Well yes, we did. One morning when Gr — when his wife had taken all the children swimming." She looked down into her cup with a return of that reluctance which came upon her every time the subject of homosexuality came up. "He said that this Timothy Wycliffe wasn't a bad man, but he was trying . . . well, to push him in that direction, if you see what I mean. And Andy said things built up in him till he felt that — I don't know — that frustrated, that mixed-up that it all spilled over into violence. Our Andy was never a fighting boy, though he could stand up for himself if he had to, but he wasn't a great talker either. I think maybe he couldn't argue with him on his level, and because of that it all built up inside him. It's as simple as that."

It sounded as if it had elements of truth, but I didn't believe it was as simple as that.

"But he repeated that he didn't kill him?"

"He certainly didn't kill him! You've got to believe that. He was alive when Andy left the flat. I don't think you understand what sort of a boy Andy was — still was when we got to know him again, was all his life. I suppose by the lights of a man such as yourself he wouldn't be considered particularly intelligent — though he was good at his job. What he was was straight. That's why I loved him. That's why lots of other people loved him too. He was good to people — loyal, helpful, generous, and I don't mean money. Wasn't it your boss the last Prime Minister said that the Good Samaritan had to have money? ”

It was my turn to squirm.

“That may not have been the best thought-out of observations,” I murmured.

“Seems a funny sort of Christianity to me. Seems to me what made him good was the fact that he stopped and tried to help. Andy was that type. He always had time for people, listened to them, did what he could for them. He was kind and patient and considerate. Now, you’ve read up the facts of the case, haven’t you?” She was looking at me very intently, pleadingly. I nodded. “Well, I ask you: can you see a young chap like that, when the man he’s been fighting is lying senseless on the floor, taking something heavy and bashing his head in?”

I suddenly made a commitment.

“No,” I said.

There was still an hour to go before the pubs closed when I left number thirty-five. I had given Mavis Nicholls my phone number as I left, in case anything occurred to her that she had forgotten to tell me. Nothing would, of course. She was a reluctant witness: her brother was innocent, but she simply didn’t want the matter brought up again. I wondered if I might get a different perspective by talking

158

to her neighbours.

As a minister I had got out of the habit of going into pubs. In fact as a minister one got out of the habit of doing a lot of perfectly normal things. It's not just lack of time, it's the danger of being buttonholed and harangued, not to mention blown up. The Duke of York was a nineteenth-century building, honouring presumably the man who later became George V: there were mirrors with brand names of whiskies and cigarettes on them, a lot of brass, but though plush would have completed the picture it had been replaced by green plastic. The man behind the bar served me with all the respect due to a man who has ordered a double Scotch.

"Haven't I seen you somewhere before?" he asked, I thought with more than the nominal welcome to a new customer.

"I shouldn't think so. It's my first time in the neighbourhood. I've been visiting Mrs. Nicholls down the road."

"Oh yeah? Friend of yours?"

"That's right."

"Nice woman. Her hubbie's a barman too — down at the Dog and Whistle, just near the station."

In books he, or someone propping up the bar, would immediately have started talking about her brother Andy. In real life a bit more helping-on was needed.

"Sad life," I said.

"Don't see what's sad about it."

It was in fact the man propping up the bar who spoke — a man just next to me, watery-eyed and droopy moustached. I put him down immediately as the resident whinger: the no-one's-had-a-harder-deal-than-I-have type. But he was sixty or so — the right age for my purposes. He went on, working himself up: "Her husband's got a job, hasn't he? Lost his old one, just like me, but he landed on his feet. I got the push when I was sixty. Sixty! You try getting a job when you're that age. They're in clover, the Nichollses, mate."

"I was thinking of the brother," I said.

"Oh, you're a friend of Andy's, eh?"

It was said with an incipient leer. He really was a very unpleasant old man.

"No, I'm afraid I've never met him."

"You're better off not meeting a shirt-lifter like that one. Mind you, I was at school with him and nobody never suspected he was a pooftah, not then. I expect it was these London queers as got to him. Anyway, I don't see what's tragic about Andy Forbes. He got away with murder, didn't he? Did that bloke in, and then got clean off. Them days he could have been strung up, 'stead of living the life of Larry in America."

"I was thinking of it from his sister's point of view. She was obviously very fond of him."

"Well, she goes to see him, doesn't she? It's no different from if he'd emigrated to Orstralia. Better, because it's nearer and nicer. I tell you, mate, I wish I had a relative in America who'd pay for me to swan off on holiday there."

"Ah yes, she said she did once go there."

"Once? She goes there every two or three years. Sometimes Les goes with her, sometimes one or two of the children. He's fallen on his feet, that's for sure."

"Andy? But I thought he was dead."

I didn't, but I thought it as well to stick to the official line. The man shrugged.

"First I've heard of it if so. Mavis was out there last year, so it'd have to be recent if he is. Mind you, Mavis Nicholls would never say."

"She doesn't talk about her brother round here?"

" 'Course she doesn't. Use your loaf, mate. Would you talk about him if you had a pooftah brother who'd killed his nancy friend? According to her she goes to visit a cousin. Doesn't fool anyone. Did you ever hear of a cousin as generous as that? No, it's Andy, and whatever he's doing he's doing well out of it. Don't tell me he's had a sad life, nor

161

her either. They don't know the meaning of the word trouble."

Before he could define it for me, with examples drawn from his own experience I hurried in with: "Still, he can't come back to this country."

"Who'd bleedin' want to?"

He had pressed in me the button marked "politician," and I was about to launch myself into a spiel about the transformation we have wrought in this country's fortunes and so on and so on, when I realized where I was and what I was doing and held back.

"Any idea what he does in America?" I asked.

"Search me, mate."

"Or where he lives?"

"No idea. She's very cagey about that, plays her cards close to her chest. That makes it even more sure it's Andy she visits. She says they travel around when they're there."

"No specific towns?"

"Wouldn't mean much to me if they'd said. I couldn't tell Oklahoma from New Orleans. They have mentioned things they've been to. . . ."

"What sort of things?"

"Empire State Building, Space Museum, Golden Gate, that sort of thing."

New York, Washington, San Francisco.

That wasn't going to help much. My companion was off on his grievance.

"It's obvious he's not wanting for the ready, isn't it? Standing them holidays like that. A pooftah kills his boyfriend, and that's how he ends up. Talk about luck — some people scoop the pool."

I bought him a drink and took my leave. I'd had enough whingers in my constituency surgeries to last me a lifetime.

11

The GREAT and the GOOD

On the train back to London, after one of those hotel breakfasts where you help yourself to a selection of near-cold victuals, I did some thinking. My first conclusion was that Andrew Forbes is still alive. If he were dead, why would his sister give the date of his death as 1988 when she had apparently visited him in 1989? Of course it was just possible that she had visited his widow and children, but I remembered her saying about the letters he wrote home: "He still — right up to the time he died — sent them to her." To me that seemed an odd, if cleverly improvised, formulation. I believe the sentence started out as "He still sends them to her," and was hurriedly modified.

There had been another place where she had pulled herself up. That was also when she was talking about letters from America. She had said that the police would be suspicious of them *especially* with his — and at that point she had changed tack and said something feeble about his being on the run. I felt sure that she had been going to say something like "especially with his name on it having the same initials" — or the same initials in reverse, or something of that sort. People who have to choose false names for themselves are notoriously prone to choosing ones which have some connection with the original ones, as if that original name were part of their personality which they can not bear entirely to obliterate. There had never been any suggestion that Andrew Forbes was a man of any imagination, and I guessed this was what he had done. Of course he didn't have to put any name on the envelope, but aerogramme forms and most American airmail envelopes have a special place for the sender's name and address, and an unsophisticated person might take it to be obligatory to write it. So he had sent the letters to friends down the road, and later to his married niece.

It seemed to me, now that I was getting a fuller view of the murder and its investigation, that the police had not made any great effort in this case. Oh — it was not surprising that by now the thing was as dead as a dodo: that would be normal, for all the police cant about never closing a file on an unsolved case. But *at the time* . . . It would surely have been

165

a simple enough matter to get a look at the incoming mail of the Forbes family and their closest associates. I had a sense of the police, once they had decided the murderer was Andy Forbes and that he had left the country, washing their hands of the case. The interesting question was why? Was it a feeling that having to live abroad rather than wonderful old England was punishment enough for the poor beggar? Was it a feeling that this was a quarrel between two queers, just what one would expect, and who cared? That would have been pretty characteristic of some police attitudes at the time, though a vengeful itch for persecution was a more common one.

Or was it political pressure?

Had there come down from on high a message — doubtless a whispered confidence from someone at the Home Office — a message which in cultured, confident tones said: well, the case was solved, wasn't it? Was there anything to be gained by pursuing this young thug any further? It would only cause a lot of added grief and embarrassment to the victim's highly respected family . . . and so on. The unspoken subtext being: to his highly respected family who, quite by chance, happened to be represented in the government of the time. I do know how these things work. The Macmillan government was conscious of the danger of scandal long before the Profumo affair. There was a whopping one very close to the Prime Minister himself, after all.

I rather suspected that this was it; that if there was a lack of zeal among policemen in the pursuit of Andrew Forbes, it was because of a few whispered words from on high.

So I concluded provisionally that Andy Forbes is still alive and well and living in — where? Not Santiago anyway. I had my own ideas about that, and I was willing to bet that when I checked up in my atlas on my return home I would not find any Santiago in the U.S.

I turned out to be half right. There was no Santiago there, but there was, I found — squinting, even with my reading glasses, at the horribly small print of the *Times Atlas*'s index — some Santiago Mountains in Texas, and a Santiago Park in California. Mrs. Nicholls had mentioned taking the children to Disneyland, not Disneyworld, which probably indicated the West coast, though in view of other places they apparently told people they had visited that was not conclusive. Still, the state of California had acted as a magnet, in the decades since the war, to a host of way-outs and undesirables, as well as to some very desirables indeed, so my attention kept coming back to the West. Santiago Park was to the south of Santa Ana, apparently also a mountainous area. Whether Andrew Forbes had ever lived there, or his sister had ever visited it, I did not know. What I did think was that Mavis Nicholls had begun inadvertently to say the name of the place where her brother had lived, maybe still did live, and that she — an unpractised liar, lying for love — had then changed it for another town whose name was very close in sound. I believed that the place that she had just stopped herself from naming was San Diego.

I wondered about San Diego. I knew from my Defence Ministry days, '79 to '80, that it was very much a naval town, with a yachting fraternity well to the fore. This might mean that there was quite a distinct British community there. That might make things easier for me — or more difficult, if Andy Forbes was a member in good standing, and they clammed up.

I rang Reggie's home in Los Angeles tonight, but I miscalculated the time again, and got only the answering machine. I loathe those things, like all right-minded people, but against my better judgment I put the phone down, got my thoughts together, and then rang his number again.

"Reggie," I said when the recorded message finished, "get me a good private detective and tell him I want him to find this man: his original name was Andrew Forbes, his current name will either have the initials A. F. or F. A. He has an American wife, probably called Grace, or possibly Greta, and at least two children. He works in the electrical business and he lives in the San Diego area. I suggest the British community there might be a help, if they're approached tactfully. Love to Helen and little . . . Howard."

Better not to talk to Reggie. He'd probably want to know how much of the above information was factual, and how much based on guesswork. I felt a load had lightened on my shoulders, and I was glad not to have my optimism shattered. I went down to dinner and chatted with Jeremy about the City (a subject that now bores me inexpressibly) with excellent grace.

Today I went to morning service in Rochester Cathedral.

I have to admit that these days I am only an occasional churchgoer. That may seem like hypocrisy, since all the time I was a constituency MP I was a pretty regular attender, and this influenced two of my children: both the twins, Fiona and Christopher, are very committed Christians, and inclined to regard me as a backslider. Very well then — I am a backslider and a hypocrite.

I did not ask Jeremy to come with me. I doubt if he has been inside a place of worship since he left school.

As a prelude to going to Rochester, which I knew I would be doing sooner or later, I have taken up *Edwin Drood*. I had in any case given up *Philip* — or it had given up me: its wittering verbosity after a time went straight in one ear and out the other, leaving not a wrack behind. *Drood* is no masterpiece, but it is much more engaging and it gives an added point to my visit, and an excuse for it which I thought might come in useful.

After a good breakfast cooked by Nina I drove down there. Sunday is the only day when driving is any pleasure in the London area these days. The weather was fine, and I enjoyed pottering around the High Street, the gate-house, and the close, where the Dean enquired after Mr. Jasper's nephew. I had taken the precaution of ringing the Diocesan secretariat and ascertaining that the Archbishop of Canterbury's special adviser on urban affairs would be conducting the service that Sunday. A quarter of an hour before it was due to begin I went into the wonderful old building and found a place towards the high altar. Uncharacteristically I sat on the aisle, directly in view of the pulpit.

I wanted to be noticed.

I tried not to mock the service of worship by treating it purely as a means of observing the Archbishop's special adviser. When he first came in I was genuinely at prayer, asking for guidance in my public and personal life. Some minutes later I got an excellent view of Lawrence Cornwallis in profile: it was an impressive one — regular, fine-drawn, ascetic, set on a tall, lean body. He had a distinguished presence, yet he gave off no impression of arrogance or intolerance. Rochester — sleepy, self-satisfied Rochester, as Dickens saw it — had been lucky to get such a man, even if it presumably only got a marginal amount of his time and attention. Here was one of the Great and Good that one did not have to be cynical about. Such, at any rate, were my first impressions.

The service he conducted veered in the direction of High — shall we say in political terms fifteen to twenty degrees right of centre? His sermon was short, trenchant, relevant, and beautifully spoken. It was at the end of the sermon that he noticed me. I could see that he recognised me, as I always know when people recognise me in the street — a mere flicker of the eyelid will tell me. In the past I would flash a politician's smile when this happened. Now I no longer do. I saw Lawrence Cornwallis later in the service cast another look in my direction. I wondered about his position in Rochester, and whether he would shake hands and mingle after the service. I thought he probably would, and almost certainly would today — not out of any desire to fawn over a politician, but from a sort of courtesy: his views might be radical, but I suspected his personal standards were old-fashioned. A visitor of some note should be singled out and welcomed. At the end of the service I lingered a little, savouring the spaces through which John Jasper's voice had echoed, at least in Dickens's imagination. Then I went out with the last of the congregation.

He was there — not exactly shaking hands with a line of worshippers, but mingling with them, exchanging greetings and enquiring after families. He had fairly clearly been keeping an eye out for me, for when I emerged he came up, arm outstretched, and smiling with what seemed like genuine friendliness.

"Mr. Proctor! Nice to see you here. I recognised you in the congregation."

"It's the television," I said apologetically. "Politicians could be quite anonymous before the box was invented."

"Very good thing. Makes you more accountable. What brings you to Rochester?"

"Oh, a fine Sunday and the prospect of a

pleasant drive," I lied. "And I happen to be reading *Edwin Drood.*"

"Ah yes. We get a regular trickle of Droodists. And are you an Edwin dies or an Edwin survives man?"

"Ah — you put me on the spot. I haven't quite finished the re-read, but I think I'm an Edwin survives man."

"So am I. It's a pleasure to meet a right-thinking person. Have you seen the Close?"

"I have, but I thought of taking another turn there before I left."

"Good, you're in no hurry. You can come and take a glass of sherry with me."

"How kind."

"I'm interested that a retired minister should be — reduced, I almost said, which would be blasphemy locally — should feel the need of the *Drood* mystery to occupy his time."

"Harmless, though, don't you think?" I countered with, as we entered the Close. "I don't think you've been an enthusiast for the government I used to be a member of, so you should rejoice in so harmless a hobby for me."

He smiled acceptance of what I said.

"I work a lot with young people, and certainly I can't remember a government that has harmed the interests of young people as this one has." He said it seriously, but I did not respond. I lost my taste for political argument the day I lost office. He smiled, acknowledging my silence. "I can see you might not want to talk about it. I don't blame you. Our last Prime Minister had a one-track mind. And it was a very narrow-gauge track." He ushered me towards a door. "My house — my 'residence.' No Droodian associations, I'm afraid."

He took me through to a sitting room of elegant proportions, though of no particular distinction in the furnishings — probably it had in fact been furnished by the Church Commissioners, whose anonymous taste did little credit to men who were guardians of so wonderful an architectural heritage. On the wall, on the other hand, there was unmistakeably a John Piper (one artist I can recognise), and something I suspected might be a Sickert.

"Younger son," Lawrence Cornwallis explained. "My brother got all the loot, and I got a few favourite pictures. Quite right too. I've never had much idea what to do with money."

He went to a bookcase in the corner and began pouring two glasses of sherry from a single bottle. I was reminded of my long-ago visit to Lady Thorrington, though this sherry, like Marjorie Knopfmeyer's, was unremarkable in quality. There was about Lawrence Cornwallis an air of sophistication that would not have been out of place in the Belgravia of the fifties — though it was not a worldly sophistication that he had. I think perhaps the word is not sophistication but distinction. He had a spiritual distinction that was palpable. Oddly enough his next words took me back to the Belgravia of my young manhood.

"I think you've forgotten," he said, "but we've met before."

The politician in me took over.

"Met you? Oh I say, do forgive me: you know in political life one meets so many —"

He was looking at me with a quizzical smile.

"Oh no — before you went into politics, at least in any big way. We met at a small party in Timothy Wycliffe's flat."

I looked at him hard. The tiny smile was still there. I was very glad the subject had come up, but I couldn't remember meeting him, and I couldn't remember any party. Old men forget — that's the only explanation, for I have been trying very hard these last few weeks to retrieve all the memories I had of Timothy.

"As far as I remember it was an after-work party," said Cornwallis. "I think a sort of farewell to you. There were a lot of Foreign Office people there, and a few friends of Tim's own."

"Good Lord!" I said. "You're quite right. Now I'm beginning to remember."

"I was one of Tim's friends, of course," he said, gesturing me to a seat, perhaps to give me a chance to hide any embarrassment I might feel. "And by the way, to get the topic out of the way — and how it does come up as soon as Tim's name is mentioned! — I've been celibate for many years. Since I decided to enter the church, in fact. Others make different decisions, and I don't blame them, but that was mine. I thought I'd better tell you, since the topic does so hang in the air whenever Tim and his death come up. A lot of people are a bit uneasy on the subject of gay clergymen."

"I'm not upset by it. Why should I be?"

He raised his eyebrows and looked at me closely.

"Well, I see you at service, clearly knowing what to do, and I assume that as a practising member of the Church of England you have views on the subject."

This was said with something of the same quizzical smile I had seen on his lips earlier. I got an odd, uneasy feeling that I had been rumbled.

"I'm afraid that much of my Church of England worship was merely formal — the local MP doing his duty. I lack the faculty of reverence or worship."

"Was this why you were sacked from the government?"

We both laughed.

"Two of my children have it," I hastened to add. "The faculty for worship, I mean. My twins, Fiona and Christopher. Fiona is studying for the Church — whatever you let her do — and Christopher is in the Sudan on an Oxfam project. But I'm afraid they must have got it from Ann, my wife. I am essentially secular. . . . It's odd you should bring up Timothy Wycliffe . . ."

"Yes?"

"I've been thinking a lot about him recently. Writing my memoirs seems to have brought him back to me, and now I can't get him out of my mind. Particularly his death."

"Ah yes, his death." Cornwallis nodded, his eyes narrowing as if in pain. "His death haunted me for many months. I'm not sure it didn't have something to do with my entering the church. It seemed to me then so terrible — and also so surprising."

"Ah, you too. Why?"

"People — people in general — often are unsurprised by violent deaths in homosexual circles — deaths like James Pope-Hennessy's for example. They seem to think it goes with the condition. That's nonsense, of course. It's only unsurprising if you're a homosexual with sadistic or masochistic tendencies, someone who is turned on by violence. I never saw the slightest evidence that Tim was one of those."

"Did you come to know him very well while you were living in his flat?" I asked.

"Ah — you know about that: not as well as you might expect. I was between bed-sit and flat of my own at the time, and the invitation to spend the ten days I was to be homeless was a piece of casual friendliness to someone he knew only slightly — carnally, it must be said, but slightly. This was at the time when the whole Suez business was starting — when would that be? — around July, fifty-six. Colonel Nasser had just announced the nationalisation of the Canal. I think Timothy was caught on the hop, but it meant even then that he was working twelve hours a day or more. That meant I saw very little of him."

"You say Tim was caught on the hop — but he wasn't on the Middle Eastern desk of the F.O. when I was there. He wouldn't have had any special responsibility for responding to Suez."

"Sorry — I expressed myself badly. I gathered from conversations while I was staying in his flat that he was thinking of resigning his job there, but that when Suez came up there was so much extra work — for everyone, because of the need to coordinate reactions in the West — that he felt he couldn't."

I frowned.

"I had heard that Tim thought of resigning from the F.O. at the time of the invasion, but I hadn't heard of his intending to so much earlier."

"You resigned," Lawrence Cornwallis pointed out. "Was Tim altogether happy and at home at the Foreign Office?"

"Well no, certainly not. He was much too much of a free spirit. But what, I wonder, did he plan on doing?"

"I've no idea. Perhaps go into business, like you."

"I shouldn't think so. That's no more a place for a free spirit than the Foreign Office. In my case it was meant as a prelude to an entry into politics."

"Maybe in his too."

"I doubt it. He was essentially apolitical. People often tried to push him into politics, Conservative politics, of course, but he always managed to sidestep. I remember him once saying that in the fifty-one election he nearly voted for Anthony Wedgwood Benn, as he then called himself, because he was so dishy, and the only reason he didn't was because he felt he was unreliable."

We both laughed.

"He was very acute," said Lawrence Cornwallis. "Not always in his own affairs, of course."

"You mean the boy who killed him?"

"No — no, I didn't mean him, actually. What I meant was that anyone who is as promiscuous as Tim was is bound to make love to some pretty unpleasant people from time to time. They're not looking for a relationship, they're looking for sex. Just as prostitution is a dangerous business, so is homosexual promiscuity. Particularly then, when you could find yourself blackmailed."

"Is that what you think happened?"

"Before the murder? I've no idea. We weren't that close, and I wouldn't have been told. But if your question is: do I think he was being blackmailed by Andy, then the answer is that I don't. And for a very good reason."

"What?"

"I don't think they'd been to bed together. . . . Shall we go in to lunch?"

I gawped at him.

"Lunch?"

"I sent back to my housekeeper that there might be two when I saw you in the congregation. I knew you'd want a good talk. I'd heard you'd been annoying your party hierarchy by going into the death of Timothy Wycliffe."

I'd had a vague sense all through our talk that he had been playing with me. Now I knew that he had been.

"Who?" I asked.

"Told me? Wratton — Harry Wratton. *Lord* Wratton he is now, of course, now he's gone to the place I suppose you'll be going to as well before long."

"I'm not banking on it," I said wryly. "I'm not being a good boy. I suppose I should have banked on the network sending out a message on the tribal drums."

"Network?" That quizzical expression came back to his face as he carved a joint of pork.

"The network of the great and good. Or is it the network of opponents of the present government? I've known many networks since that first one I noticed in Belgravia, spying on Tim, but they all operate on a similar system: the drums sending out information and warnings to people of the same cast of mind who can decipher the drumbeats. . . . But I'm getting sidetracked," I added, as I accepted a plate of roast pork and started to help myself to vegetables. "You said you didn't think Tim had been to bed with Andy Forbes. What makes you think that?"

"Because he told me. He told me in July, when I was living there, and he told me again when I came across him by chance in the street somewhere in October. Of course it's possible the situation had changed by November when he was killed."

"I see," I said, eating and thinking. "That changes things. I've been assuming all along that they were lovers."

"Timothy loved *him* — that I'm sure of."

"You saw them together?"

"Oh yes — Andy Forbes was round at the flat one Sunday while I was staying there."

"What was your impression of him?"

"Nice, quiet lad. Sincere, kindly, rather out of his depth in Tim's kind of world."

"So how do you see the relationship?"

"I read it now as I read it then — Tim and I discussed it, you know. I don't think Tim understood the working-class feeling about homosexuality. In Tim's world it was very much taken for granted. You encountered it from school onwards. You know the story of Evelyn Waugh's friends the Lygons, and their father?"

"I've heard of it vaguely," I said. "Forced out of the country by his brother-in-law the Duke of Westminster."

"That's right. Earl Beauchamp, he was. Father of a large family, but he couldn't keep his hands off the footmen. That sort of thing would just be accepted with a shrug and a smile in the circle Tim grew up in. But it certainly wasn't in the circles Andy Forbes grew up in. There's fear, and distaste, even revulsion towards homosexuality among ordinary working-class people. I've seen it over and over again, and it's made me glad I took the decision I did, because there's so many people whom I've liked, whose views I've respected on other things, but who I know would never have been able to accept me as they did if I'd been a practising homosexual. This was something I don't think Tim understood — or at any rate, I don't think he could *accept* it. It was so . . . ungenerous that a person like him simply couldn't accept it, or believe it to be as strong as it was. So that, while I knew him, while he was in love with Andy Forbes, there always seemed to be in him . . . a sort of split."

"You mean that he was in love with this boy Forbes, but he was — to put it vulgarly — having it off not with him, but with you and others?"

"That's partly what I meant. I wasn't the main one, by the way, not by a long chalk."

"Was it Gerald Fraser-Hymes?"

"Who?" Lawrence Cornwallis shook his head. "I don't think I ever met anyone of that name. No, his main sexual partner at the time was Terry Cotterley."

"I seem to know the name."

"You would. He was secretary for a long time of the Hatherley Trust — the pressure group that agitated for a change in the laws on homosexuality. One saw a lot of him on the box in the late sixties, when the law was changed. Eventually he became one of the 'great and good' as you call us — though that would have been unimaginable in the fifties."

"I'd like to talk to him."

"Died of AIDS, two or three years ago."

"Ah," I said. "Things are not *that* much rosier for homosexuals now than they were in the fifties."

"That's right. I've had to argue with people who believe it's a God-inflicted plague, punishment for the sin of sodom. One does wonder sometimes what kind of God such people imagine. . . . Some more pork?" When he had helped me and himself to more, he said: "Oh, by the way, when I thought you might be coming I looked through my old photographs."

"Photographs?"

I felt excited. I had never thought to bring up the possibility of photographs, even with Tim's sister.

"Yes — I thought there probably wouldn't

be many of Andy Forbes lying around." He went over to the desk-bookcase under the window of the dining room and, coming back, handed me a snapshot. "It was the Sunday I mentioned. We went up to Hyde Park, to swim in the Serpentine. I was rather a keen photographer then. We got a passer-by to take that, though."

It was a group of three, all in flannels and white or check open-necked shirts. Tim stood with his arm around Andy's shoulder, and the young Lawrence Cornwallis stood a little apart, as I imagine that, mentally, he always stood. All were laughing boyishly, and there was about them a sort of innocence, which may seem odd, but is perhaps a comment on the fifties, vis-à-vis our own times. I peered into the face of Andy Forbes, but I could see no trace of murderer, no sense of outrage or resentment: I saw only the carefree pleasure of a healthy young man on a fine summer's day.

"*Now,*" said Lawrence Cornwallis in a determined way, "if you've no more questions I want to talk about homeless young people."

"And how was he, this Special Adviser to the Archbishop?" asked Jeremy when I got home. He had spent Sunday playing squash.

"Not at all what I expected. I'm afraid I

185

rather look on the Church as somewhere where people can gain position and influence without possessing talent. And I'm always suspicious of the great and good. But Lawrence Cornwallis is genuinely impressive."

"Oh, by the way," said Jeremy, the light of mischief in his eye, "there was a phone call just before you got home. It was Lord Warboys. He obviously thought I was you — we have rather similar voices —"

"South London flattened."

"Maybe. Anyway he rang off when he found out who it was. But I gathered he wanted to sound you out on whether you would go on some Royal Commission on Regional Development."

"Could be interesting," I said.

"More likely deadly beyond imagining, I'd have said. Anyway, don't go on so about the great and good. You're in danger of becoming one of them. You're a sort of political Tom cat whom the vet has operated on."

I suppose that is one of the consequences of being a retired cabinet minister — a sort of political neutering takes place. I looked at Jeremy affectionately.

"You're so good for my ego," I said.

12

PARTY POLITICS

It is strange how much one can remember simply by an act of will. I had not realized that before, perhaps because my life has been one of doing (or appearing to do) things, leaving little time to chase memories. The only time I remember doing that was soon after Ann died, one evening when the children had all gone their ways: I sat, I recall, in the living room, going through our life together, putting those last cancer-ridden months aside and trying to get a grip on the good years of our marriage, the births, the holidays, the anniversaries, hoping that she had been happy.

Now, this Monday morning, I sat in my armchair in the study and went into a long, fiercely willed meditation in which I tried to bring back all the details of that farewell party in Craven Court Mews. I had always been aware of the fact that I had been to Tim's flat on other times than that first embarrassing visit when I had so pathetically revealed my gaucheness and conventionality. Now I realized that the most important of the other times had been Tim's farewell party for me. How ungrateful of me to forget it. Gradually, little by little, details of it began to pop up in my memory. I was in such a deep brown study, submerged in that time, that I actually jumped when Jaime showed Elspeth in.

"Don't get up," she said breezily. "Go on thinking great thoughts. I've just got a pile of stuff on the collapse of the Heath government and your part in it."

"I didn't have any part in it!" I protested, jumping into my instant-politician stance. "I was only the most junior of ministers at the time. I thought calling a snap election was madness. It was Carrington advised him to do that."

"Well actually it's mostly election speeches, with you saying it was the only honest thing to do." She seemed to take a mischievous delight in telling me that. I sometimes wonder whether Elspeth is a Conservative at all — or even conservative. Or is she just cynical from having worked on too many politicians' memoirs? "Oh, by the way," she went on, "I'm on the track of Gerald Fraser-Hymes."

"Splendid."

"Nothing definite yet, but I think you'll find he's an industrialist in the Midlands. I should have more concrete info next time. Now you can go back to thinking great thoughts."

"Actually I was remembering a party, on the day I left the Foreign Office, whenever that was."

"January 27th, 1956," she said promptly. "It's ringed with red in your diary. You must have been pleased to go."

Yes, that was part of my memory of the time: I had been pleased to go. I had not enjoyed working under Eden. There were some who were very fond of him — and some, rather more, who hated him. I was too junior to be close enough to love him, and I certainly don't think I hated him. But I was very uneasy about him generally: he often treated his subordinates abominably, and he seemed to have the prima donna reactions some people get when they have been in politics for a long time. I think I had some forebodings that there was something in his character that would lead him, and perhaps the country, to disaster. I had decided to resign even before he became Prime Minister. The advent of Selwyn Lloyd as Foreign Secretary at the end of fifty-five was the last straw. Industry, I saw, was a much better stepping-stone than the Foreign Office to a career in politics, and when I got the offer of a very good job with I.C.I., I accepted joyfully.

"You're quite right to go," Tim said when I told him, "quite right. We're both outsiders here."

"Outsiders?"

"Me because of my sexual preferences, you because you didn't go to a good enough school." I must have shown my surprise, because he went on: "They may not make that clear to you, but they certainly make it clear to each other."

He was quite right. I had been blind not to have noticed it before. You needed to go to the top four or five schools really to be acceptable to the F.O. hierarchy. The snobberies of Lady Charlotte Wray were the snobberies of the Foreign Office — the Foreign Office then, and for all I know the Foreign Office now. None of my various government posts were there, and I was glad: it would have been too much like going back, and I never like to do that. Quite apart from the fact that I would be thought not to have gone to a good enough school.

So Tim determined to have a little party for me, independent of any brief and tepid gathering that might take place at work (I remember none, but I expect something of the sort must have been put on by my immediate boss there). It had to be after work, because it was Tim's mother's birthday, and he had family commitments. It was, I now realize, her last birthday, and probably the family knew that it might be.

Tim had invited seven or eight Foreign Office people — one or two I was close to, the rest people I had worked closely with — vague figures now, who played no part in my later life. The only one I remember at all vividly was Bernard Wriothesley, who later had a variety of diplomatic postings, including one in Bucharest — he was, I believe, the man who recommended that honorary knighthood for the late Nicolae Ceausescu. He was ambitious, bright up to a point, but none too sensitive.

Tim's friends arrived in dribs and drabs, collected drinks, and mingled with the F.O. crowd. Often the two groups knew each other, having been to the same schools, or because they were in with the same set. It was an all-male occasion, which nobody seemed to find odd. I wish I could say that I remembered Lawrence Cornwallis there, could recall any words I swapped with him, but I can't say that I do. Perhaps, impressive though he is now, he was not impressive then. Wordsworth, I have often thought, was quite wrong about the process of growing up: the child is not father to the man, nor even the young man to the mature man. Lawrence Cornwallis left no trace in my memory.

Other things, though, I do recall.

The tone of the talk I remember: it was catty. People often talk about the cattiness of homosexuals, but it is nothing to the cattiness of the people in the F.O. The latter deliver it on a much lower note — from the back of the throat, as it were, with the lips scarcely moving, and with a face blank of emotion. It could be devastating.

The talk began innocently enough: Eisenhower's prospects of reelection, the new broom which (then as now) was apparently transforming Russia. The F.O. men did not think much of Khrushchev — "a peasant" they pronounced him. I went around from group to group, feeling myself on the outside even when I was most in on the talk. Perhaps Tim's remark about how people in the F.O. regarded my school had made me uneasy — though he had not said it unkindly, or to have that effect, quite the reverse: for Tim Foreign Office people were worth being on one's guard against.

When Tim's friends predominated, the talk tended to be more arty: the new regime at Covent Garden, *The Mint* which had just been published, the film of *Richard III* ("Wonderfully camp!"). Again, I felt a little bit on the outside looking in. But I do remember that, with Tim dashing backwards and forwards fetching and refilling glasses, proffering plates of things to nibble, it was possible to talk about him, and I remember it was the Foreign Office contingent that did it most enthusiastically. To be specific, it was Bernard Wriothesley, gazing down a long, beaky nose and looking around him with a circumspection that must have served him well later in Romania.

"The sad thing about Tim," he said with relish, "is that he's never going to get very far up the ladder. How could he? Would you regard him as a good security risk?"

"I don't think Tim bothers a great deal about getting ahead," I remember saying. This was the first time, as I recall, that Tim's sexual orientation was openly discussed in my presence. I was, out of friendship and because of Tim's caution, extremely guarded.

"Precisely my point. If he had any ambition he would be a whole lot more discreet — as many *are* whom I could name but won't. Tim is essentially a dilettante. That father of his robbed his children of ambition — he has so much that there's none left over for them. And *he's* a sparrow who thinks he's a nightingale."

"I don't know Tim's brother and sister," I said neutrally.

"Oh, I believe the sister's a lively little thing. She'll no doubt marry someone suitable and never be heard of again. Women never get anywhere in the Conservative Party. I was thinking of the brother, Brother James, frère Jacques. *The* most boring man, with a dreadful horse-faced wife. Ghastly managing sort of woman. If she gets her way James will rise to the dizzy eminence of Deputy Lord Lieutenant of Gloucester, or wherever they live. A nothing man. And Tim — who certainly isn't a nothing man — will *amount* to nothing in the end. Such a waste. Frightfully sad."

"All you mean is," I said, "that Tim will amount to nothing in the F.O. Probably you're right. But there are other places to distinguish yourself. F.O. men always forget that."

"We prefer not to think of them. Obviously you have to feel that way, being on your way to the big bustling world of commerce." (How he curled his lip as he said that!) "But the F.O., let me tell you, is what Lord John, Tim's dad, has his eye on. Probably sent Tim to us as a stalking horse. But he'll never get it, not Tim's papa."

"Why not?"

"Well, I could say too mediocre, but with Selwyn Lloyd as Foreign Secretary that might not ring true." He threw back his head, withdrew his voice further into his throat, and prepared to give us a potted biography. "The fact is, he was too compromised in the thirties by his association with the Cliveden set. That was Lord John's habit — they seemed the way of the future, and he latched on to them. If Churchill and the rearmers had seemed the way of the future he would have thrown in his lot with them. As it was he went a mite too far: much too pally with Ribbentrop, talked in a public speech about Hitler's miraculous transformation of Germany — you know the sort of thing some of that lot did. Of course he became a super patriot during the war, but people don't forget. So he'll never rise above the mediocre jobs his talent fits him for, which I suppose must be a cause for gratitude. Certainly he'll never get the F.O. Which doesn't stop him *wanting* it fiercely."

The talk turned back to Tim. Maybe I should have moved away, but there was a sort of grisly fascination in hearing Tim's assessment of his position within the Foreign Office confirmed in his own flat by people who were accepting his hospitality.

"Mind you," said Bernard Wriothesley, looking around him circumspectly once again, and bringing his hushed tones from some shadowy recess in his gullet, "if he *were* to get the F.O., he'd find young Tim more of an embarrassment than an asset. He doesn't get any wiser in his choice of friends."

"This lot," said another of the F.O. guests, a faceless man I cannot put a face to, "is the public face. The private one is by no means as acceptable. Plumbers and bricklayers and jazzband singers — all sorts of riffraff. Beggars description. God knows where he picks them up."

"There's one of his best friends," breathed Wriothesley, "who's about to start a public campaign. To get the homosexuality laws changed. Now of course everyone agrees that those laws are positively medieval —"

"Oh, absolutely. Barbaric. Still —"

"Still, a public campaign's hardly the way to go about it. Right . . ." He nodded wisely. "A few words in the right quarter would do a lot more good. Personally I think a suggestion from the Home Office to the police that they lay off for a bit might work wonders. The laws might just shrivel away, without there being any great *fuss*. No *publicity,* that's the point. But you know what these queers are like: fuss is exactly what they enjoy."

"Horribly high-pitched, most of them," agreed the faceless man. "And absolutely unreliable."

"Oh, absolutely."

This was in 1956, seven years before the Profumo affair. The greater reliability of heterosexuals would have been more difficult to argue after that little business. At the date I am remembering, though, the Conservative Party hadn't had a major sex scandal in decades. Imagine Baldwin with a call girl! So homosexuals were fair game for Bernard Wriothesley, though he did have a faint idea that he had just contradicted himself with his wild generalisation, because he added: "Though as I said earlier there *is* another way of going about it. Think of —"

He named a high-up in the Foreign Office whom everyone regarded with quite breathless awe. I had that delicious feeling of delighted discovery that being in on gossip always gives one: I had never even thought of the man in a sexual light at all. Then I felt guilty about my delicious feeling, and grubby by association.

Any other memories I have of that gathering are no more than fragments. I recall someone saying "Tim's riding for a fall," and someone else saying "Of course all Belgravia is chattering — a rich, discreet buzz." I also remember a chat in a corner alone with one of Tim's friends in which he said: "The climate's changed since Guy Burgess, hasn't it? The F.O. protected him for years. That couldn't happen today. The first whiff of scandal about Tim and he'll be out on his ear, won't he?" I remember that I nodded miserably. The Foreign Office had been subjected to so much criticism and ridicule after the Burgess-Maclean affair that it could no longer afford to have as its first priority the protection of its own.

"Well, I hope Tim does get out before that happens," said his friend.

My last memory is of helping Tim to collect up glasses and stash them in the kitchen before he went off to the family bash for his mother. By then people had gone, drifting off in ones and twos. We were alone and working at high speed, but at one point I remember I was collecting up dirty plates from the handsome glass and rosewood table I had admired on my first visit when I noticed that a Delft vase was sitting in the middle. It seemed incongruous — too delicate, too old-fashioned in taste. I said: "Not your sort of thing, I should have thought, Tim."

He looked at it and smiled sadly. "Present from an unhappy woman."

And that is the sum total of my memories of that party. I sat there in my study, collating and sorting them, wondering what Tim had meant: was Tim's mother congenitally unhappy, or was she unhappy about Tim, or what? The reverie was interrupted by the phone ringing.

"Peter Proctor speaking."

"Yes, well, Mr. Proctor, I'm not going to pretend and be polite, because I feel very bitter about what you've done to me."

My heart sank. I knew the voice and could guess the grievance.

"Mrs. Nicholls, I —"

"You knew I wanted it all to be discreet, you knew I'd asked you to come after dark so the neighbours wouldn't see you, and what do you do as soon as you leave this house? You go straight down to the Duke of York and start talking about Andy."

"Mrs. Nicholls, it was just casual conversation."

"I'll thank you not to treat me as a fool, Mr. Proctor, because I'm not that. Did you really think no one in the pub would recognise you? And that when they did, it wouldn't be all round the pub as soon as you went out of the door? Now everyone in the neighbourhood is talking about Andy again, and why an ex-cabinet minister should be interested in him. The whole street is buzzing, and people are looking at me sidelong. It's just like 1956 all over again."

"Mrs. Nicholls, I was just trying to help."

"Don't give me that. Funny way of trying to help, making sure it's all raked up again. Well, don't think you can rely on me. Don't imagine you'll get any more help from me.

As far as I'm concerned you're Andy's enemy, and I'll act accordingly."

There was nothing to be said to placate her. And of course she was quite right. I had simply ignored her feelings and wishes. I'm afraid years in government may give one the impression that one can simply ride roughshod over others. I had not thought — and if I had I probably would have done the same. I was sorry, and felt bruised. Yet I was sure of one thing: she would never have been so angry, nor have talked in those terms, if her brother were not still alive.

13

CAPTAIN of LIGHT INDUSTRY

The Portland Metal Box Company was situated ten minutes from the centre of Leicester, in an unlovely suburb that accommodated several other light industrial plants that contributed substantially to the unloveliness. I had taken the train to Leicester (I have loved trains since our family outings to Westcliff-on-Sea as a child before the war). At the station I took a taxi, and as usual I asked the driver to set me down some way from my destination, the Metal Box Company. The driver was Asian, and didn't want to talk about football. I paid him off, walked about a little, sniffing atmosphere: postwar semis, council houses, several rather anonymous pubs, a long street of shops: supermarket, chemist, video shop, off-licence, wine bar, Chinese takeaway, Italian restaurant — the standard enterprises of Britain as it lurches into the nineties. There was a dank anonymity about the place, a sort of nothing-very-muchness that was depressing, speaking of limited ambition, dashed hopes. But of course this was not where Gerald Fraser-Hymes lived, only where he worked.

Elspeth Honeybourne came up with the gen on him two days ago. Most of it was gleaned from local newspapers, for Gerald had certainly never been a national figure, but she had also discovered information in the old boys' section of a school magazine, *The Margrovian*. How she had got on to that I have no idea, nor where such a publication would be kept, but it turned out that Gerald Fraser-Hymes had gone to a small private school outside Cheltenham called the Margrove Towers School (not an establishment, I imagine, that would have impressed the men at the Foreign Office). Gerald was an enthusiastic old boy, communicating to a breathless if small world his various doings: his third-class honours degree, his becoming army ski champion of 1959, a minor military citation for service in Cyprus, civvy street in the early sixties, with a variety of jobs in a succession of large and small industrial firms. An undistinguished life, culminating in positions of responsibility on Chambers of Commerce and local branches of the Confederation of British Industry.

But what turned out to be most useful was a photograph that Elspeth had found in the *Leicester Evening Clarion*. It showed officials of the South Midlands Light Industry Federation at its annual dinner-dance: six portly males surrounding their president, Gerald Fraser-Hymes. One might have got the impression from the photograph that the males danced with each other, but that I thought was unlikely. Fraser-Hymes was slimmer, shorter than the others, but wearing an expression of determined bonhomie and confidence in himself and what he was doing. It was the face, the photograph seemed to say, of a successful and contented man.

That photograph gave me a stroke of luck — though there was an element of calculation at work too: I have to admit that I dawdled around the Portland Metal Box Company's entrance for some time, conscious that it was coming up to lunchtime, so that when I saw a group of sober-suited men coming, talking and laughing, from what seemed like the administrative block in the middle of the plant I dallied by the wall, watching and waiting, apparently poring, head down, over an *A to Z* guide of Leicester.

Gerald Fraser-Hymes was in the centre of the group, and at the centre of the talk and laughter. His voice was loud, perhaps cultivatedly so, and his laugh hearty. The other men, as in the photograph, were bigger than he (actually I recognised one of them from the photograph), but Fraser-Hymes seemed to be some kind of leader: they didn't defer to him exactly, but they seemed to respect him, accord him some mild eminence. They turned left at the gates, and headed towards the row of shops, still loudly discussing and laughing, and very much occupying the pavement.

I had a bet with myself that they were off to the wine bar, but I was wrong: they turned into the little Italian restaurant, da Paolo, where I could see through the glass door that they were ushered towards a reserved table. I waited a minute or two and then followed them. The place was decorated with plastic vines and pictures of Tuscany. It aimed at intimacy, but achieved only nondescriptness. However it had the advantage of being small enough for all the tables to be within earshot of Fraser-Hymes's party. I indicated to the waiter a dark corner table, from which I could study the party with impunity. As I glanced through the menu they were ordering two lagers, two pints of bitter, and a glass of white wine. Though I was not hungry and seldom eat much at midday, I decided I had to stay at least as long as they did: quite apart from anything else there didn't seem to be anything better to do in the vicinity of the Portland Metal Box Company. I ordered stracciatella and bistecca pizzaola, with a half bottle of red wine. Then I took out the *Spectator*, put it on my side plate, and prepared to watch and listen.

Fraser-Hymes had a pint of bitter in front of him, and he ordered turkey breast Bolognese with a mixed salad. From the description of the dish in the menu this seemed to indicate a taste for rich food warring with a desire to stay slim. I soon gathered from the conversation that one of the men with him was his second-in-command at the works, while the others were local businessmen from other small firms. The talk, though it was interspersed with broad jokes and loud laughter, was about business, and the doings of the South Midlands Light Industry Federation. Not surprisingly it was not, as conversation, invigorating: "How does this scenario look to you, Tony?"; "There's going to be a lot of fall-out from that one, Gerry"; "Pete's not going to accept that without a dingdong battle" — that sort of talk, meaningless to an outsider, and not particularly meaningful to an insider.

It was when I was starting on my beef pizzaola that the talk at the next table became a little more personal.

"Ah," said one of the bulky businessmen — Pete, Tony, or whoever — responding to some proposal of Gerald's, "now there just could be a bit of a problem there." He forked a piece of creamy veal and mushroom into his mouth, chewed it, and then bent his substantial frame over the plate and addressed Gerald in a hushed but still beautifully audible voice: "Now, Gerry, I don't know if you noticed at the dinner-dance — a lot of people did — er . . ."

"Notice? I probably didn't. I was pretty busy."

"Of course, of course. Very well you organised it too. We-ell, the general murmur was that there was something going on between Frank Warner and Harry Goldsmith's wife."

"Really?"

"Nothing concrete, you know — nobody caught them behind the door in the cloakroom — it was just a sort of tension: both of them very aware of each other, know what I mean? Little glances you had to be damned sharp to catch. . . . Anyway, that's the whisper. Right, so if you put Frank in as secretary and Harry in as president, then if something *were* to blow up . . ."

"Right. Absolutely. Point taken. So what do you suggest? Hold back Harry's presidency till ninety-two?"

"That's the ticket. I'm sure you can think

up a cover story, Gerry. Ninety-two, year of opportunity — that kind of thing. Then we could have Dave Barton as secretary. No danger of Dave straying from the straight and."

"That wife of his wouldn't let him off the lead long enough," said another, wiping his mouth. "Handsome woman, but you can pay a price for that sort of good looks. . . . Oh boy, marriage! You've got the right idea, Gerry, old boy!"

"Right idea, Jim?" Brief, knowing smile.

"Keeping out of it. And when's the next of these famous weekends, eh, Gerry?"

"Weekend after next."

"London here you come. Put out the flags in Soho."

"I'll just be taking in a show or two." Again the same smile.

"Showgirl or two, more like. No, there's no doubt about it: you've got the right idea." He shook his head, preparing to impart a profound piece of wisdom. "I tell you, in the old days, when your eldest son followed you into the business, then there was a point in marriage and a family. Not any longer. Your sons sneer at you, go off to university, where they expect you to support them, then off to some job in the City screaming share prices at a computer screen, where they earn fifty times what you do, and patronise you when they do condescend to come home for the weekend. No, marriage and family have had it. Gerry here was ahead of his time. . . ."

They went back to eating and drinking, and talking about Pete's sales figures and Harry's cash-flow problems, and when this new Chancellor would get inflation under control and interest rates down. It was the sort of talk I've heard a hundred times in my lifetime. The only time they reverted to the personal was at the door, when Gerry and three of his lunchtime companions said their goodbyes.

"If I don't see you before the weekend after next, Gerry old boy, have one on me, eh?" The tubby man poked him in the ribs. "Or two or three, if the fancy takes you. By heck, I envy you. Chance'd be a fine thing, eh, Tony?"

And uttering a series of these coded clichés, these verbal totems, they vanished into the dreary afternoon, Gerry taking off to the left with his second-in-command, the rest going the opposite direction. I ordered coffee, to give Fraser-Hymes time to settle back at the office, then I paid my bill and followed him.

There was no security to speak of at the gate of the works, and I walked through and went straight to the small, uninviting administrative block — the sort of not-really-trying architecture that characterised the whole area.

When I asked the girl in the outer office if I might see Mr. Fraser-Hymes I handed her my card. She took it without interest.

"Do you have an appointment?"

"No. I thought he might see me without."

The girl glanced up at me. My face seemed to ring more bells than the name on my card. She reached towards the telephone, then changed her mind and slipped out through a door at the side of the office. There was a ripple of whispering, then I was conscious of being watched through a slit in the door. A moment or two later the door swung open.

"Mr. Proctor! This is an honour. I don't know what we owe it to, but you're very welcome."

He was all smiles and handshake. His breath smelt of beer and peppermint, but his eyes were clear and sharp, and close to I had the impression of someone who kept himself in good physical shape. He ushered me through to his office as if this were a proud moment in his professional life (poor fish).

Once there it was difficult to know how to start. I couldn't convincingly say that I happened to be in the area (it wasn't an area one could happen to be in), and I wasn't going to pretend to be doing a survey of the fortunes of small companies and how they were coping with high interest rates. Luckily there was no immediate need to put my cards on the table. Gerald Fraser-Hymes had ordered coffee, and he filled in the interval as best he could by producing the sort of waffle that a retired politician meets wherever he goes.

"Sad day when you resigned from the government . . . well, sacked if you prefer . . . moderating hand at the tiller . . . of course they still have my wholehearted support . . . this new business rate, on top of the Poll Tax, is losing you friends in droves around here . . . member of the local association . . . not as active as I'd like to be, but you know how it is . . . filling in the time pleasantly enough, are you? Directorships, Royal Commissions, that sort of thing?"

He ran out of steam, but he'd given me an opening.

"A bit of this, a bit of that. But much of the time I'm writing my memoirs."

"Look forward to them."

Liar.

"I'd better tell you why I'm here. Back in the fifties we had a mutual friend: Timothy Wycliffe."

He stiffened — perceptibly, involuntarily.

"*No.* . . . No, I can't recollect knowing anyone of that name."

"You stayed for a time in his flat near Belgrave Square. That's not the sort of place one would forget staying in."

The tension in his body was palpable.

"No, you've got the wrong chap, I'm afraid."

"I don't think so. I don't believe there could be many Gerald Fraser-Hymeses of the right age. . . . Look, could we stop playing games? I should emphasize that I'm not in the least interested in your private life —"

"What's that supposed to mean? What are you implying, eh?"

He was looking immensely fierce, like an outraged colonel, but the fierceness seemed to be genuine. He was talking in a low voice, almost a hiss, but this did not detract from the angry intensity of everything he said. I sighed.

"Mr. Fraser-Hymes, I'm not trying to accuse you of anything or blackmail you. I've quite simply become interested in the death of Timothy Wycliffe. I'm just asking you as a friend of his —"

"That's the trouble with you politicians: you get so bloody arrogant you think you can barge in wherever you like and ask whatever questions you feel like asking. Even a police officer would have to have a bloody warrant! Well, this time you've got it wrong. I'm under no obligation to talk to you, and I'm not going to. You can just clear out!"

"Very well," I said, getting up. "But I can't see what you're upset about. You talked to the police at the time."

He spluttered. The girl came in with plastic cups of coffee. She looked at Fraser-Hymes's face, put the cups on his desk, and fled.

"So you've been getting at police records, have you?" he resumed, still talking in a hiss. "That's what people mean when they say this government abuses power. You've no right to go digging into police records of thirty-odd years ago. All right, I'll tell you this — what I told them at the time: I was nineteen in 1956. I'd just left school and I was studying at London University. I couldn't find digs because my parents were so bloody close with their money there wasn't anything I could afford. Wycliffe offered me a room, and I lived there for a few days, until I cottoned on to the filthy things he and his pals were doing, and the filthy things he wanted me to do with him. Then I got out. That's it, and that's all!"

"While you were there, did —"

"No! That's it. That's all I've got to say. Now get out."

So out was what I got. I have to say I admired him. What he did took bravery — not because I am at all a formidable person, quite the opposite, but because someone who has been a cabinet minister and a sort of B-team

212

national figure does acquire a certain aura that means people address him with respect, accord him a certain dignity. It is, if you like, a cut-price version of the divinity that doth hedge a king. To order me out of the room demanded bravery.

That in other respects he conspicuously lacked bravery might be argued, but one must remember his age and his occupation. To have "come out" in the world of industry and commerce — what would have been the effect of such a gesture? The ridicule would have been unimaginably crude, the understanding and support virtually nil. His position would have speedily become untenable. He had made his decision: he had settled for an existence of dirty weekends in London, a façade as a marauding bachelor with tastes that the boys could understand. In his small world he had done a really good job of self-defence, had produced a protective camouflage that really did protect.

I did not believe him, obviously. I did not believe Timothy would have offered any young man a room in his flat, even for a short time, without having made his own sexual orientation clear. It was overwhelmingly probable that Fraser-Hymes was one of his boyfriends. Further than that I would not go. It did not seem to me that the man's reaction was that of a murderer — even one whose crime lay way back in the past. It was, quite simply, too belligerent. The natural instinct would surely be to be apparently cooperative, with a great deal of misleading flimflam and a lavish supply of red herrings. Though he lied as to fact, his reaction to my enquiries seemed basically an honest and spontaneous one. . . . On the other hand, of course, I had caught him on the hop with a subject he must have thought had been buried decades ago.

You note that I have begun to consider the people I talk to in the light of potential murderers.

14

The MAN in QUESTION

I don't think I've ever seen a town or city I disliked more than Los Angeles. I have seen Blackpool and Belgrade, Burnley, Oslo, and Bombay, but none of them is so horrible a nonplace as Los Angeles. It is like being part of a nightmare future, and my instinct after ten minutes in the taxi was to tell him to turn round and take me back to the airport. Not, I imagine, that changing direction is possible on those roads. You will say that I did not come prepared to like the place, but then who does? The reputation of the city has gone everywhere, and the reputation is the truth.

The message had come from Reggie while I was in Leicester. Jeremy had been at work, and the message as taken by Jaime read, "Dective thing he found Fobbs." I interpreted this to mean that the private detective had found a man he thought might be Andy Forbes. I rang Reggie, got Helen his wife, and she confirmed this, adding that they'd be delighted to see me any time I cared to turn up. I said I'd turn up just as soon as I could get a plane. Jeremy wasn't due back till late in the evening, so I wrote him a long and affectionate note in explanation, which I was sure he'd just skim through and crumple up. Then I simply packed a few things and rang for a taxi to take me to Heathrow. There are always seats on some plane or other that is going to the States.

The man in the seat beside me on the plane to Chicago wanted to talk about how high interest rates were affecting industry. I told him I'd put all that sort of thing behind me now. I realised suddenly that that wasn't just an excuse — it was the literal truth about how I feel. All that was another life. We talked about his grandchildren instead. At Chicago I overnighted at the airport hotel (if you opened the window you got the most concentrated dose of diesel fumes I've ever experienced), and the next day I caught the early flight to Los Angeles.

Reggie and Helen live in a fairly "nice" part of Los Angeles — that is if you could forget the town itself, the polluted atmosphere, the trip Reggie had to take to work every day, and the rubbish on the thousand and one television channels. I really fear for my grandchild. I don't know Helen well — I've seen her before only once since I flew over for the wedding — but I like what I know. She gave me a warm welcome, introduced me to Howard (who doesn't look in the least like a Howard, much more like a John or a Charles), and for much of the day until Reggie came home from work we all three played outside in the "fresh air."

Later that evening, over bourbon and water (a very comfortable drink which I could get a taste for), Reggie and I talked. He had had a recent letter from Christopher in the Sudan and he filled me in there; I brought him up to date about Fiona as far as I could, and of course we talked about Jeremy. One thing I'll say about my son: he's a very good listener — very patient and understanding. I don't suppose he has much to do directly with insurance customers, but he's the sort of person one feels one can't lie to or conceal anything from. I said to him:

"This Timothy Wycliffe business is becoming a bit of a mania. Or perhaps a haunting would be a better word — I'm haunted by it. I feel I have to get it off my back before I can do anything else."

"Is there a book in it?"

"Do you know, I wondered that? It sounds a bit heartless — a sort of bloodsucking — a blatant misuse of a friend's tragedy. On the other hand I thought it might do good. But at the moment I'm not sure I have *any* book in me, let alone that."

"Of course you have a book in you, Pops. You're the most intensely bookish person I know."

"That's not at all the same thing. The memoirs are coming out as dead as last year's turkey."

"But perhaps a book about Wycliffe's death would be more interesting to write. You would be more involved. And, let's face it, everyone loves an unsolved mystery."

"Whereas no one loves a politician's memoirs? You're probably right, though it's often puzzled me how many copies some of them seem to sell. Still, I'm afraid mine will fall into the instantly remaindered category unless I produce a lot of catty revelations about the PM, and that I'm determined not to do."

"Still running scared even now she's gone?"

"Not at all. It's a question of honour. But I must admit that the thought of a book about Timothy's death is much more attractive, at the moment, than plodding on with the memoirs."

"The private eye I hired is pretty sure he's got the right man. He swears he was extremely discreet, and there's no way the chap could have got the wind up."

"I suspect that's irrelevant now. Andy Forbes's sister took offence at my going into the local pub and asking questions. Quite rightly, I'm afraid. It was a stupid and insensitive thing to do. I'd guess that she's almost certain to have alerted him by now."

"You don't think he'll have taken flight?"

"No — if I've got the man right I don't think he will have. What name is he living under now?"

"Frank Andrews."

"I thought it would be something like that — a simple reversal of initials and a terribly ordinary name."

"All the information is in the file," Reggie said, handing it to me. "When will you go?"

"I think I'll go tomorrow. But maybe I'll go by train, stay a night or two, try not to rush it. I don't want to talk to him in a state of jet lag."

Reggie went away and booked me a seat on Amtrak and a room in a hotel. Rather nice, really, to have got to the stage where one's children do things for one. In spite of my having been a cabinet minister I'm sure Reggie feels I could barely survive in America on my own. The next day he made sure he not only took me to the station, he practically put me on the train. It was in fact a beautifully clean and safe-making train, and I couldn't imagine what ghoulies and ghosties he felt he was protecting me from.

The Ulysses S. Grant has a silly name (or perhaps I mean the president had a silly name), but otherwise it had everything I like in a hotel and never these days get. I decided to bask in its comfort and friendliness and not to rush things. I needed to think out my approach to Andy Forbes. I walked around the older parts of the town, soaking up atmosphere — the atmosphere that was so lacking in Los Angeles — and thinking through what I knew of Tim's death. Basically I could guess what Andy Forbes was going to tell me — if he told me anything. And on the whole I stood by my commitment to his sister. What interested me was the character of the man, and what had moved him to act as he did. I believed that if he did talk he would be honest.

Nothing would persuade me to drive in the States, so hiring a car was out. There was no option but to take a taxi to the address given in the folder Reggie had handed me. (The report, by the way, was admirably full, specifying the length of time Frank Andrews claimed to have been in the States — over thirty years — and details of his wife Grace and his children, his business career, and so on. The report mentioned the visits every two or three years of his sister, either with her husband or with one or other of her children. It said specifically that he had no criminal record, nor did any of his associates in the San Diego area have any suspicion of a criminal past. The report was signed Noel P. Rosegarden, which struck me as an odd name for a private detective — though no odder than Pinkerton, I suppose.)

I asked the taxi to set me down ten numbers short of Frank Andrews's address, and stood waiting for him to drive off. It was rather a pleasant area — prosperous if not affluent, each house surrounded by a good garden, plenty of trees, with a view out to the intense blue of the Pacific, where yachts and warships mingled peaceably and the sea melted into the sky. The houses themselves were one-story, unimaginative but comfortable — looking not unlike the houses in Australian suburbs. The air was warm but fresh. I walked slowly down, watching and listening to the sounds — commercial radio here, children playing there. Slowly I approached 1468 Riverside Drive, taking my time, keeping cool and collected. Like the other houses, it was a one-story, with a little archway over the front door and a laburnum tree in the small patch of front garden. A low hedge surrounded it in the English manner, and I walked past the gate and round the corner, so that I could see it had a good stretch of lawn and flower beds at the back, as well as a stunning view of the harbour. I walked along by the hedge, taking in the flowers and shrubs, the air of peace and comfort. I stopped with a start when I realized the garden was not empty.

A middle-aged man was playing in a sandpit by the back door with a small child. He was stocky, well set-up, and only just beginning to gain flesh. He was playing tenderly with the tot, but when I involuntarily stopped his eye was caught. People walk around less in America, and I think that was what made him look at me — our eyes, in fact, met. There was a pause of just a second or two as I wondered what to do, and then he got up and walked over, extending his hand over the hedge.

"I think you must be my fate," he said.

For all my resolutions about keeping cool I found myself totally at a loss, as once I was years ago when I was accused on television of lying, and all I could do was splutter. Faced with his calm directness all I could do now was mutter "not at all" and "please believe I have no intention —" My idiocies came out as splutter. He was the one who was cool.

"You must be Peter Proctor."

"That's right."

"My sister sent me a newspaper picture."

"But you never thought of . . . taking flight?"

"Good Lord, no." He gestured deprecatingly. "I'm much too old to take flight. I've lived with this a long time, and always at the back of my mind there was the feeling that one day, somehow, somebody was going to come up and confront me with it. Do you know I've never once been recognised in the States? Not a tourist from Nottingham saying I reminded him of someone, nor a technician from the BBC scratching his head and wondering. I'm glad it's happened like this — something big, a confrontation, rather than something awkward and petty. Oh no — I'm not running away."

He spoke with an American accent, but it may have been the sort of accent, like Alistair Cooke's, that sounds American to British ears and British to Americans. Certainly there was the odd expression now and then in his speech that reminded me of his long-ago origins. It was an attractive blend — but there was a great deal about the man that made me think I understood Tim's feelings towards him. There was a tough, uncompromising side to him, but there was also, still, that blinding honesty that his sister had spoken of. I suspected that he had done well in business, but not *too* well: the honesty, beyond a certain point, would have prevented that.

"I'll let you in the front door."

I walked round and he let me through a house that was well, but comfortably, furnished, with family mementos and photographs dotted everywhere — on shelves, television, piano. There was a conventional but convincing painting of a pretty woman hanging over the fireplace that I took to be his wife.

"Grace has taken the older grandchildren to the aquarium. I'm standing duty with Emma. We're lucky — our eldest girl is married to a naval man and lives in San Diego. Something to drink? Coffee? Beer? Orange juice?"

"Orange juice sounds like a good idea."

He put some halved oranges into a fearsome machine, which after great heavings and groanings produced a glass of rich yellow liquid. He put sugar in it and handed it to me.

"Who exactly are you?" he asked. "I'm sure I should know, but I don't. And what is your interest in this?"

It was said in that direct, honest way that made me uncomfortable.

"I was a cabinet minister until a year ago. I worked for a time with Tim in the Foreign Office. I'm writing my memoirs, and it was that that got me interested in his death."

"Did I ever meet you in the old days? Were you one of his boyfriends?"

I shook my head. Both of us, miraculously, were perfectly unembarrassed.

"No, I was never that. But I was a friend. I think Tim trusted me."

He nodded and led the way out into the garden. He took two toys from a little pile, and went down on his haunches and tenderly started the little girl playing with them. He waited, watching her, then took me over to a garden seat and sat down.

"Tim trusted me too," he said. "That's a bitter memory to have. . . . Surely Tim can't figure in much in your memoirs? He was never an important man."

"No. It's not that he was important to me in a political sense —"

"He wouldn't have liked your government, would he?"

"No. . . . It's more in a personal way he's important. . . . His presence disturbed me, if you can understand that. The memory of him — his gaiety and honesty — wouldn't go away."

Andy Forbes nodded, looking down the length of the garden and the years.

"You know, for years now I've tried to think of him as he was earlier, not . . . not on that last day. I think that's what he would have wanted. . . . Yes, I know people are always saying that to justify doing any damned thing they feel like doing, but I *do* think that's how Tim would have liked to be remembered. Tim was never morbid, didn't dwell on things . . ."

"Tim accepted things — himself, other people," I agreed.

"People here — in America, in California in particular — love analysing themselves, going to shrinks, getting into groups for therapy. It doesn't seem to help them very much. Me, after a time, I just said: that's something that I'm going to have to put behind me. It was heartless, maybe, but necessary. And I have put it behind me. That's why I can remember some of the happier times with Tim."

"Is it difficult to talk about?"

"Yes. . . . Very difficult."

"Shall I ask questions?"

"We can try it that way. I don't know if you'll ask the right ones — the ones that might make you understand."

"Where did you meet?"

"That's easy. A theatre in Leicester Square. They were showing *The Man Who Knew Too Much*. Tim had seen the earlier version — he went to film clubs and that, I just went to the pictures. Anyway, we started talking."

"Was he chatting you up?"

"No . . . Yes . . . It's difficult to say, really. He probably chose the seat next to me because he liked the look of me. He probably had bed at the back of his mind because it usually was. No disrespect to him. But he was also genuinely friendly, genuinely enjoying chatting with a stranger. Certainly as far as I was concerned I was just chatting with a nice fellow."

"So he didn't make any . . . sexual signals?"

"If he had I wouldn't have received them. As far as that went I was completely green."

"Yes. I was the same when I first knew Tim."

"So that was it. We had a drink afterwards in a pub in St. Martin's Lane." He smiled reminiscently, as if he was talking about another world. "Of course I'd realised by then that he was completely out of my class. If I was bothered by anything — if I felt at all awkward about being with him — it was about that. That's why I was surprised when he telephoned."

"*He* contacted *you?*"

"Oh, of course. I'd never have thought of contacting him, though he did give me his card. He rang me at the BBC. . . ." Andy Forbes paused and thought. "I said just now I was completely green as far as homosexuality was concerned. Thinking it over that can't have been so. I don't just mean playground jokes. I'd naturally come across it at the BBC. People brushing against me once too often, the hand on the behind, the veiled invitation. But that was always showbiz people — *obvious* homosexuals. You could either laugh or get aggressive, but it was all sort of outside you, not part of your life. With Tim it was different."

"Yes. I felt that."

"Gradually we started going around a bit together — films, football matches, restaurants. I went to my first live play with Tim. I took him round his first television studio. And I went to his flat . . . It was like another world."

"Did you feel jealous?"

"Jealous?" There was no hesitation in his vigorous shake of the head. "No, I'm sure I didn't. You couldn't be jealous of Tim. I think I just thought: I'd like something like this one day."

"I think some of the boys he picked up did feel jealous."

"I wasn't a boy he'd picked up. I was a friend. I knew Tim. I knew he worked hard, didn't flaunt his money . . . In fact, I never knew if he was wealthy or not, only that he'd inherited this flat in a posh part of London."

"And all this time there was no sex?"

He turned to look at me.

"How did you know that?"

"Someone told me."

"The newspapers had a different story. It upset my family no end. . . . But it's true. There was the odd advance — sort of 'why don't you try it?' — but I just stamped firmly on it and said I wasn't interested. But of course I knew by then that he was a homosexual, and that he slept around a lot."

"And that didn't worry you?"

He thought for a moment before answering.

"I think it must have. I enjoyed a lot going around with him, being taught about films, food, living the high life in a mild sort of way. But I think it did worry me, because I remember saying to one of the guys at work: 'There's this chap I know who's a homosexual, sleeps around like nobody's business. They'd clap him in jail if they could get him on a charge.' I shouldn't have mentioned him. After that there was a lot of jokes about arsebandits, poofs, pressure on me to prove I was one of the blokes, hetero as they come. You know how it is. . . ."

"Yes. But there must have been pressure from Tim in the other direction."

"Not at first. We went around, I met his friends — some of them I liked, some disliked, as you'd expect. The ones I disliked tended to be lame ducks he looked after, or limpets. I even met his sister one night — a lovely girl. Tim was very fond of her, like I was — am — of mine. . . . I was enjoying myself, enjoying life . . . Then —"

His face was screwed up. He was obviously finding this difficult.

"Yes?"

"Then I realized he was in love with me."

"How?"

"Looks. The way he treated me compared to the way he treated the guys he just slept with casually. Eventually he told me: 'You do realize I'm in love with you, don't you?' "

"How did you react?"

He smiled shyly.

"What was that old stand-up comic's line? 'I don't wish to know that.' It was a bit like that, though I was — or thought I was — a lot more sophisticated then than when I'd come up from Nottingham. I think I said: 'I know. I'm sorry, but it's no go.' "

"You didn't think about stopping seeing him?"

"No. I suppose you find that surprising. I think I stood him up a couple of times, to cool it, but no. I liked him. . . ." He put his head in his hands. "Of course I know now that's what I should have done. God knows I know it now! Everything would have been different . . . but then it hardly occurred to me."

"When was this?"

"When it came out into the open? Oh, about a month before the . . . before it happened. Tim was very busy at work, I remember, and for a week or two that helped to cool it. But he was also very mixed up with a pal of his, a chap called Terry Cotterley, with plans to set up some kind of — I don't know — club or organization, to press for reform of the law on homosexuality."

"Yes, the Hatherley Trust — a sort of pressure group."

"Oh, did it get set up? I didn't know. Anyway, I wasn't too happy about that. Seemed to bring it all too much out in the open for my liking. I wondered whether I wouldn't have to drop Tim if he did go and work for them. . . . Anyway, cooling it didn't really work after a time. Tim was still working at full pressure — it was the lead-up to Suez — but any free time he had he'd telephone me, get me to see him. I was sorry for him. He was like a kettle that was boiling away and no one would take it off the stove. He was against the Suez thing, but he was working for the government that was doing it. . . . Then there was me."

"Was he pressuring you?"

"Yes . . . Yes, after a time that's what he was doing. Pleading with me to 'try it.' Saying I just couldn't understand it if I hadn't done it. That he knew I was fond of him, and that it was natural to go to bed with him, if only to please him. All of it was true in a way, or true for him. I was so sorry for him. I was really torn apart. That's how the situation was the day he died."

He jumped up, his face gleaming with sweat. "I need a drink."

15

The NIGHT in QUESTION

He scooped up his grandchild from the sandpit and went into the house. I remained on the seat in the sun for a minute or two before following him. He was holding the child effortlessly on his shoulder and pouring himself a drink.

"Want one?"

I nodded. He poured from a bottle of bourbon and handed me the glass. The little girl on his shoulder started whimpering, made restless by his restlessness, and he put her on the floor. Then he fetched her a soft toy, gave it to her tenderly, and stood watching her for a bit. I wished I had a grandchild I was as familiar with, and as good with. When she was playing away happily and crawling around the floor with her bear he gestured towards two armchairs at the shady end of the sitting room.

"That day began like any other," he said, nursing his glass in his hand. "It was a Thursday. There had been people living in Tim's flat on and off over the summer —"

"Lawrence Cornwallis and Gerald Fraser-Hymes."

"Right. I think I remember the names. I have a picture of Fraser-Hymes in my mind as a rather furtive man, not at all Tim's type, except that he didn't have types, and made friends of all sorts — friends and lovers. . . . Anyway, there was no one living with him at the time, but he was expecting Terry Cotterley over. Soon after I arrived — mid-morning — Terry phoned to say his mother was ill and he wouldn't be coming, so we were alone for the day."

"How did Tim come to have a free day?"

"He'd been working practically twenty-four hours a day for two weeks, including the previous weekend. Nearly everybody at the Foreign Office had been, he told me. Tim said he'd been given the day off because they didn't trust him and they were planning something really underhand, but I think he was partly joking. So we went as we often did to Hyde Park, and we talked."

"What about?"

"Oh, Suez, of course. Being given this day off made Tim think they didn't consider him reliable. Not just because he was against it — lots of people in the F.O. were that —

but because he was a homosexual. It didn't actually worry him very much. He was intending to resign. But he did want to talk about it. Oh, then we got off that subject and talked about this trust thing that Tim was going to work for . . . but all the time I was conscious of pressure."

"On him or on you?"

"On me. Well, both, really. Tim was under intense pressure — I'd never known him so tense — and walking with me in the park was a way of letting it escape, relaxing, refreshing himself. But pressure on me too. He had me to himself, and he was going to use the opportunity. On the walk it was mainly a matter of little physical things — taking my hand, putting his arm around my waist — all very brief, because of course though it was November there were other people around. And also because he knew it embarrassed me. But it all amounted to pressure on me. . . . I felt so sorry for him."

"What did you do next?"

"We went back to the flat and Tim cooked something light for lunch — scrambled eggs, omelet, something like that. The wireless was on, I remember: a record request show on the Light Programme, with a lot of soupy love songs. Tim was relaxing, becoming so happy in my company. I knew I did him good just by being around . . . I could feel myself slipping."

"Into going to bed with him?"

"Into — I don't think I really knew what. So far there'd never been anything more than little things — the sort of things Tim had gone in for on the walk that day. If he'd tried anything more I'd pushed him away, and that had been enough. I was very naive, and I don't think I'd sorted out in my mind what I'd let him do, and what I wouldn't. All I knew was I couldn't hold him off any longer like I had been doing."

"Did Tim realise this?"

"I think so." He looked at me straight, with a sharp glint in his eyes. I was glad to see he could discuss the matter without going all shamefaced. He was a grown-up person now. "Tim didn't always get people right," he said. "He was too nice, too hopeful. But about bed he was very sharp. He was terribly happy over lunch — radiated it. Then he cleaned the plates away. I went on sitting there. Suddenly I felt his hands on my shoulders, and down the front of my body. I thought: this is it, and I let myself be taken into the bedroom and undressed. I don't think I ever saw Tim so happy."

Andy Forbes took a big swig of his bourbon and stood up, walking around the room, playing for a moment with Emma. What bothered him I suspected was his own violence, not his sexual encounter with Tim. When he came back he was calmer.

"You won't want a description of what happened next. At any rate I'm not going to give you one. I don't think I know any longer what my feelings were — whether I liked it, whether I hated it. It's been blotted out by what happened later. I know we were in bed for two hours or more, and that Tim was ecstatic, even when he was just holding me. He told me, and I could see it, feel it. Eventually we got up, talked about other things, walked to Victoria Station to buy some cigarettes, did a lot of very trivial and normal things. We came home and listened to the news — there'd been tremendous uproar in the House of Commons that day. And all this time, when I was apparently behaving normally, something was building up in me, and Tim didn't know it, didn't even sense it."

"What was it? Revulsion?"

"No, not that. I don't think it was that. But it may have been a sort of . . . resentment. I think it began when I lay there with him in bed. I thought: this is it. I've done it. I've crossed the river of no return. That's what it felt like. And the next thing I thought was: he pressured me into it. It wasn't my will, it was his. I think I did love Tim in a way, but it wasn't that way. It was his personality, his style, his funniness. He *was* lovable, but I felt he'd used that, consciously — used it to make me do something I didn't want to do. That's why I felt resentment."

"Did you feel . . . cut off, in a way?"

He nodded vigorously.

"*Yes*. That's what I did feel. All the time we were making love it was there, festering up inside me — this feeling that it was he who had made the choice for me, and that now I was somehow apart. I began thinking of my family. You may think that's pretty pathetic in a man of — what was I? — twenty-four. But I'd always respected my mum and my dad, accepted what they believed in. I wasn't someone, then, who thought things through for himself. They were decent people and I tried to imagine myself going home to them and saying: 'Look, I'm homosexual, and I'm sleeping with this guy whose father is in the Cabinet' . . . It was just fantastic, impossible. Yes, I know, it's something a lot of people have done, especially these last years, but I couldn't have done it, couldn't have told them. And if I couldn't tell them, what did that say about what I'd just been doing with Tim? . . . All this is bloody naive, I know."

"Not at all," I said. "It's probably how I'd

have felt too at that age."

"Then, just before we had dinner, there was this phone call from Terry Cotterley. A new idea for this pressure group he and Tim were setting up. And I sat there listening to Tim talking and I thought: 'This is me, this is my future.' A special case. Someone who people snigger about in pubs, someone who has to press for what he does to be made legal. A minority. It was as if at a stroke I'd been cut off . . . was adrift. Someone a bit apart from everyone else — friends, family — because what he does is different. I'd always seen myself as an average guy, and now suddenly I wasn't. . . . I don't pretend I was thinking clearly. That was the whole problem — I couldn't. Now, when I try to put it into words it sounds wrong, because I wasn't a words person then, and what I'm describing was a gut reaction. It was all welling up inside me, and it all came back to that feeling that a choice had been made for me, and it wasn't my choice."

He got up and poured himself another drink. I had barely touched mine.

"The next bit is even more difficult to explain."

"The fight?"

"It wasn't a fight. He didn't resist. I beat him up."

He came over and sat down again, looking bleakly back through a long time-tunnel.

"We ate — steak and salad. We washed up. I went and sat down in one of the armchairs. The conscious part of me was saying 'I want to go home. I want to think this over.' But underneath that there was only this great swirling mass of feelings — resentment, anger, feelings of betrayal, of having been tricked . . . a sort of black rage. And when he came over behind me again, like the first time, and bent down and kissed me and asked me to come to bed, I shouted: 'You don't know me at all, do you?' "

"What did you mean? That he didn't understand you?"

"Partly. That he couldn't understand my feelings — my prejudices, if you like — because he came from another world. He said: 'Of course I do. I understand. It's strange first time, but you did enjoy it, and you'll soon get used to it.' And I shouted: 'I won't get used to it! You don't understand me. You don't understand how I feel. You say you *love* me, but you don't *know* me at all. You don't know how I'd feel about people knowing, about my family knowing.' He went on fondling and said: 'Why do you have to think all the time about other people?' And I thought: 'It's easy to ignore what other people think about you when you have money, self-confidence, position . . .' "

He stopped, and I said nothing, letting him take his own time as he looked back down that dark tunnel.

"He ran his hand down my body, and when he . . . when he got to my prick I was seized by a blind rage. I jumped up and I turned round and I hit him — savagely across the head. That ought to have been enough to release me from the rage, but it wasn't . . . I somehow couldn't stop. I kept shouting 'You don't know me — you don't know anything about me,' and sometimes, 'You don't own me.' And I kept hitting him. He didn't resist — he just put up his hands to shield himself and ran to the other side of the sofa or table. That made it worse. It was as if somehow he was saying he was better than me, had higher standards. I feel so ashamed I can hardly explain it even now. I caught him near the cabinet by the door and I banged his head against it. A vase thing fell off it and smashed to the floor. I looked at him and he was bleeding and his legs were crumpling up. He looked at me as if to ask 'Why?' and then he collapsed to the floor, stretched out facedown. . . . I looked down at him. The picture of him lying there bleeding is on my mind, like a snapshot. It comes to me in the night and I wake, sweating."

"How did you feel then?"

"I don't know . . . Not ashamed. Angry. With this self-righteous feeling that he'd asked for it."

"What did you do?"

"That's the horrible thing. Nothing. I did nothing to help. I just turned tail and banged out of the door, down the stairs and out."

"And you never saw him again?"

There was a silence.

"I saw him again. . . . I ran into the Square, then out to the Hyde Park underground. Kennington was my nearest stop, and I had a fair walk from there. I'd thought everyone would be looking at me on the underground but no one did. There wasn't a mark on me. Somehow it was that that brought home to me what a monstrous thing I'd done. On the walk home I tried to ring Tim, and got the 'busy' signal. I thought that must mean that he was all right. My landlady was watching the telly, and I got up to my flat without having to talk to her. By then it must have been about half past nine. I made myself a cup of coffee, then I sat down and I thought and thought. Eventually I felt overwhelmed by shame."

"So you went back?"

"Yes . . . first I just went out to phone

him. I wanted to say I was sorry, but that we shouldn't see each other again. It was busy again. I walked back toward Kennington Underground, trying all the coin boxes as I went. Always busy. I was getting very uneasy. I knew he was in no condition to make a long phone call. I thought he must have tried to call 999 and blacked out. By the time I got back to Belgrave Square it was well after half past ten and I was running. I had a key to the flat, and I ran up the stairs, listened at the door, heard nothing, went in, and there he was . . ."

"Dead."

"Yes. He was lying facedown on the floor, but not in the same position I'd left him in — he was just beneath the phone, which was dangling from the hook. His head was stove in from behind. He must have tried to ring for help like I thought . . . but someone had come in and bashed his head in. . . . It was horrible. . . . I went over to make sure he wasn't breathing, but I knew he was dead. I was crying. I didn't know what to do. I knew what would happen if I went to the police. Eventually I left the flat, tried to walk normally back to the tube, so as not to arouse suspicion. I think by the time I got back to my flat I knew I'd have to go abroad."

"You thought the police would arrest you

if you went straight to them?"

"I was damned sure they would. We must have been seen together during the day, my prints would have been everywhere, and one or other of his friends would dob me in. Homosexual killed by his boyfriend — it would have made perfect sense to the police, and I wouldn't have blamed them. I didn't even think of going to them. I thought of chucking myself in the river, and damned near did. Why would the police have believed me, why would they have looked any further for the murderer? It was a topping matter then. I thought of the shame to the family, I thought of my sister, whom I'd always loved. . . . I went back to the flat, went to bed for a few hours — I didn't have anything you could call sleep for months afterwards — then next day I told the landlady I was going to have a holiday before I started my new job. Then I left the country for good."

"For Las Palmas?"

"For Northern France first. I'd been there with a BBC camera crew, so I had a passport and I knew the area. I knew there'd be plenty of English newspapers on sale there. I was hoping against hope, you see, that it had been one of his boyfriends, and that he'd go to the police and confess. When I saw in the papers that the police were after me I took the train to Spain. One of Tim's friends had disappeared there when he was wanted by the police. I knew they couldn't get you back. Eventually I landed up in Las Palmas, with a job in a bar, and that's where I met Grace. That's where the nightmare started lifting, when things started going right again."

"How did you get to America?"

He grinned. The tension in him had perceptibly lessened.

"That was dead easy. Spain at that time was full of dodgy characters. Grace has been back and she says it's full of old-age pensioners playing bingo now, but then it wasn't difficult if you wanted something dicey done. I heard of a guy in Barcelona who could fix me a fake passport. I'd started using the new name as soon as I got to Las Palmas. Grace came back here, I went to Barcelona, and eventually I got a cargo boat to Mexico. Grace came down to Mexico City — her maiden name was Hernandez, and she has relatives there. We married in 1959, came here to live, and by 1963 I had my own electrical shop. Now I've got five, and I only work when I feel like it. My boy does most of the day-to-day running. . . . I belong to the local Rotarians, have a boat, and we have a cottage up in the mountains where it's cooler. It's what they call the American Dream, isn't it? . . . It's been another life. Like I've had two, with months of nightmare between them. . . . What are you going to do?"

I stirred in my seat, feeling almost guilty at having disturbed however slightly his idyll.

"Nothing. Nothing as far as you're concerned. Maybe write a book about Tim and his death."

"You do believe me, don't you?"

"Yes, I believe you."

"Then how can you write a book about his death if you don't know who killed him?"

I shrugged. I recognised the problem.

"Maybe I could leave it vague. It's Tim's life that really interests me now, the life homosexuals lived then. . . . Anyway, it's possible I shall find out."

"It's not very likely, after all this time." He had got up, and was standing by the window now, glass in hand, looking at his granddaughter. Suddenly he said: "I don't think you'd ever capture Tim."

"No," I agreed sadly.

"Not his . . . special quality."

"His distinction. No."

"He had something that set him apart, made him unique. I didn't kill him, but sometimes it feels as if I did. I know I killed something that night."

"What do you mean?"

"I think I mean that if Tim had lived, he would never have been the same afterwards. He not only loved me, he trusted me — he was sure he knew what kind of a person I was. . . . He was wrong. I killed that trust, that belief in people, and that's why it's right that I should always feel guilty."

I was just about to ask him a question when we were interrupted by sounds from the front door. As I got to my feet two boisterous children ran in, followed by a handsome buxom woman — grey-haired, smiling, dressed in the sort of smart but casual way a woman would choose who was taking young children to a fun fair.

"Sorry, Frank. Didn't know you had anyone here — I'd have reined them in a bit if I'd known."

"Grace, this is Peter Proctor, who is here from England on business."

As I went to shake her hand I caught a nod from Andy and a brief smile of contentment from his wife — two tiny signs from people clearly as close as it's possible to be. The nod told me that Grace had known about my threatened visit, and that she now knew that things were all right.

The next few minutes were bedlam. "Grandad, we went on the big dipper," "Grandad

I won this doll," "Grandad I was sick" —
all the kinds of things that children who've
had fun at a fair say the world over. I wished
again that I had grandchildren I could be as
close to and relaxed with. Perhaps one day
Fiona or Christopher would have children and
live nearby. At moments of quiet Grace Andrews pressed me to stay for lunch. I was
tempted to — the scene was so warm, and she
herself seemed so genuinely friendly and sym-
pathetic. But I knew that between Andy and
me there was always going to be a tension,
for the only thing that had brought us together
was for him a shameful, guilty memory. I
didn't know how much they saw of their
grandchildren, and I didn't want to cast a
cloud over their day. I pleaded a previous en-
gagement, and said goodbye to Grace with regret. Andy called me a taxi and saw me to
the door.

I asked the question that I had been about
to ask when the children burst in.

"Have you ever wanted to go back to England?"

He smiled. I think he was used to the question, no doubt from Americans who didn't realise that he couldn't.

"Early on I did. I desperately wanted to
see my parents again. It still hurts that I never
did. Now there's my sister, but I see her fairly

often. There's no way I could go back to Nottingham, not even if this thing were completely cleared up. It would be an embarrassment all round."

"If my book named the real murderer —" I began, but he shrugged.

"It's not an issue. What would I do? Go round all the old places I knew, see how they'd changed? I hear you're knee-deep in litter if you walk down Oxford Street these days."

"I believe it is bad. Only tourists go there."

"That's what I'd be, a tourist. No, thanks. I'm not an Englishman any longer. Everything I want is here. But good luck all the same. Tim deserves the truth. I hope you find it out."

I went out to the taxi with the sound of children's laughter from the garden gladdening my ears.

16

GENTLEMAN *of the* PRESS

The five days I spent with Reggie and his family when I got back to Los Angeles I thoroughly enjoyed. I played the grandfatherly role up to the hilt, while consenting to be led around the sights of that deplorable city. I allowed myself to be dragged to the opera on one of the evenings, and the clothes I saw then will remain with me for the rest of my life. I have to admit though — disgraceful as it may sound — that one part of me, determinedly kept down, was itching to return home and take up the case again. Perhaps this would not have been so if there had been any prospect of Reggie and his family coming to live in Britain, and my having a real relationship with my misnamed grandson. But when I brought the matter up Reggie just laughed. The only slight consolation was that there is a prospect of his moving to his company's offices in San Francisco. I have been to San Francisco and know it would provide a better atmosphere for little Howard to grow up in. But either way it seems that my acquaintance-ship with him is going to be spasmodic. So I tried to make the most of those few days, and I have to admit to having had a good time. But all the while something in me was won-dering whether anything had come up in Brit-ain, whether Elspeth or Sutcliffe had left messages about important discoveries. I have no excuse: the idea of hastening home to in-vestigate a thirty-five-year-old murder is pat-ently absurd. Yet I have to be honest and admit to twinges that I knew were an impa-tience to be back in London.

I stopped over in New York and had dinner with a literary agent who was politely sceptical about the chances of my memoirs on the American market. He gave the impression, throughout, of wishing he were elsewhere. However when, over pudding, I mentioned the possibility of a book on Timothy's murder there were slight twitches of the antennae: there's an aristocratic connection, is there? Isn't Belgravia that classy area behind Buck-ingham Palace? Political dirt is always pop-ular, though heterosex would have been better than homosex. Still. . . . Really it was quite sordid, or simply amusing, I can't decide which. But the nature of the agent's interest made me see the danger that I might write the right book for the wrong reason. That would indeed be the greatest treason.

I got back to Heathrow in the evening, and took a taxi to Barkiston Gardens. I had a splendid gossipy reunion with Jeremy over the first really good food I'd eaten for some time. He let me go on endlessly about my grandchild, and when I trailed to a stop I let him go on about City views of the state of the economy — a topic which is now infinitely tedious to me, and which I seem to have been hearing about all my life, whichever party is in power. I actually got the impression that Jeremy himself is beginning to be bored with it, which is a hopeful sign. People who make money the be-all and end-all of their lives are always punished for it by being exceptionally boring individuals whose company palls after ten minutes and repels after half an hour. I hoped for better things from Jeremy.

"Oh, your policeman rang, Dad," he said, when the topic had fallen to the ground exhausted. "I took down a message I didn't really understand."

So over coffee, with a celebratory brandy, I looked at everything that had piled up on my study desk. Elspeth had put her material in two separate bundles, and the memoirs bundle which I didn't look at was very large, while the Timothy Wycliffe bundle was small and seemed of meagre interest. Most of the letters were pretty dull too, except for two of them. There was an official-looking communication which amounted to a barely veiled threat from Gerald Fraser-Hymes's solicitors: if I brought up their client's name in any connection with Timothy Wycliffe or his death their client would be compelled . . . and so on. Interesting. Good that Timothy still had the power to shock, so many years after going to his grave. There was a letter from Christopher substantially the same as the one to Reggie I had read in Los Angeles — indeed for much of its way actually identical, because it was done on a word processor. I don't associate word processors with the Sudanese hinterland: let it never be said my children lack enterprise! Still, what a deplorable modern habit. I always put Christmas round-robin letters straight in the wastepaper basket.

I eventually came to Jeremy's slip of paper with the phone message from John Sutcliffe. It read: "Terry Pardick is the life and soul of a sunset home near Brighton. Full of stories, says the matron. Drive you down whenever you like." Now that was like being back on the trail! I rang him at once.

"Day after tomorrow?" I said.

"Right. I'll warn them in advance and pick you up at ten," he replied. "Be ready — I'd hate to be wheel-clamped."

So the next day I wrote up my talk with Andy Forbes — very methodically: I was beginning to behave like the author of a book on an unsolved murder. The pile of political stuff left by Elspeth went unregarded.

When Sutcliffe collected me he was full of his usual grievance, which I suspect he thoroughly enjoys. In the long and boring drive out of London I let him give it full rein.

"I was watching 'Coronation Street' last night, and eating this casserole my daughter Judy had brought round for me earlier in the day when I suddenly thought: 'This is *bloody* boring stew, and I could make one a hell of a lot better myself.' I could too. I'm going to invite her and the whole family round for a meal. 'Just to save you trouble,' I'll say, and I'll give them all a three-course spread that'll be a damned sight more interesting than Judy's ever brought round for me. Perhaps that will stop her. I'm the one with time on my hands, and I'm the one who enjoys learning new things."

"I must admit that in Los Angeles it was rather pleasant having my son treat me as if I were incapable of looking after myself," I admitted. "Made me feel cocooned."

"That's because you don't have it all the time. And because you're used to being

cocooned — as a minister. I'm not. I sometimes wish my daughter would move fifteen
or twenty miles further away. . . . Now tell
me about this Andy Forbes."

So I told him in detail the story, and he
nodded intelligently and probed my account
at interesting points. When I had finished he
said: "So what do you make of it?"

"I believed him. You'll have gathered that."

"Miscarriage of suspicion, if not of justice."

"That's right. Though the suspicion was
perfectly understandable, and doesn't reflect
badly on the police at the time. When I say
I believed him, I should say too that I don't
think he entirely understood himself and his
motives — not then, and not even now. I think
there was a social element — *them* with the
money and power, *us* ordinary working blokes
— and he's reluctant to admit to it out of
a sort of loyalty to Tim's memory. And then
there's his feeling that a choice had been made
for him: I think he must have enjoyed himself
in bed with Timothy, loved him sexually,
more than he acknowledges. Otherwise he
could surely have viewed it as an episode
rather than a turning point. I think these two
things added to those black feelings that he
said welled up inside him and contributed to
the ferocity of the attack. But yes, I do think
Andy Forbes is basically an honest person, and

an open and generous one, and I do think he's telling the truth."

"So what we're looking for," said Sutcliffe, "is someone who came round later and found him like that."

"Yes."

"And finished him off."

We considered this in silence until we neared Brighton. When we were chugging through the outskirts Sutcliffe handed me a map and told me I was now map reader and guide.

"I'm pretty helpless. I'm just a politician," I protested, but he only smiled enigmatically, and in the end I managed pretty well. I had wondered what sort of an old-people's home Terry Pardick was likely to have landed up in — not, presumably, one of those concentration camps named after the pioneers of the socialist movement where old people are bullied, neglected, and starved by gin-swilling, card-playing camp guards. In the event it turned out to be a large white house in a leafy suburb, with a conservatory and an open porch that caught the sun and was obviously used for sitting out on fine days. One way or another Terry Pardick seemed to have done pretty well for himself: it looked like comfort if not luxury.

"Ah yes, you're the gentlemen for Mr.

Pardick," said the first attendent we came upon, a pretty, smart young woman with a lot to do and not much time to do it in.

"He's well enough to see us?"

"Oh yes — perfectly well."

"And, er, mentally sharp?"

"Oh yes! If it's stories of his life as a reporter that you're after, you won't be disappointed. He's full of stories, is our Mr. Pardick!"

He sounded like a bore with a captive audience. The woman led us briskly through to a large, sunny lounge, with several elderly people sitting around — one or two talking, but most either reading a newspaper or watching television. A couple were just sitting and staring into space. The atmosphere was hardly stimulating, but I've never been in an old people's home where it was. As we came in most of them followed us with their eyes. What was in them? Jealousy? A cynical scepticism about Terry Pardick? I was very cautious of those eyes as we were led to a little group of three chairs set slightly apart from the others, with an old man seated in the centre one.

"Here are your visitors, Mr. Pardick."

He was a small man, in open-necked shirt and baggy trousers that flapped around him: not only small, but getting smaller. The flesh at his neck and on his hands was loose and scrawny, and his fingers were so deeply stained with nicotine that they looked like polished wood. His face was small but dominated by a large pointed nose and eyes that were sharp and sardonic to the point of cruelty. It was impossible to avoid thinking of a rodent.

When we had introduced ourselves and sat down he said:

"What's in it for me, then?"

The assumptions of the chequebook journalist died hard, it seemed. I took out a packet of cigarettes I had brought along specially and handed it over.

"Money's what I'm talking about," said Pardick, though he pocketed the cigarette packet. "You want the results of my researches on Timothy Wycliffe and I'm willing to sell."

"I'm not a newspaper reporter, you know," I said rather pompously. "I'm not after a story."

"I don't give a fuck if you're the Queen of Sheba," said Pardick. "You'll still have to pay. I'm not asking the earth. Twenty pounds will do the trick."

I said nothing, but I took out my wallet and peeled two tenners from the wad, watched by the intent eyes of every old person in the room. It may have been my imagination but they seemed now full both of jealousy and contempt. Terry Pardick took the money and slipped it into his trouser pocket.

"That's what I call businesslike. Mind you, I can't see why you're interested in Timothy Wycliffe. There's a lot bigger fish than him in my files, and pretty much for the same reason. Plenty of politicians too. When I first heard your name I thought you might be interested in some of your old colleagues — a bit of tit-for-tat for the sacking."

"I'm not."

"There was a lot of talk about —"

He mentioned one of my former colleagues who had fallen like Lucifer a year or two before I did.

"It was just talk, and anyway he's no longer in the Cabinet."

He shook his head in a horribly knowing way.

"They talk a lot about preserving the family, your lot, but they can't half put it around when they feel like it, can't they? There's that minister for —"

"The person I'm interested in is Timothy Wycliffe."

"Oh, right . . . yes. Well, it's a long time ago."

I was beginning to lose patience with him. I've always expected value for money.

"You were told that's who we wanted to

talk about. You've had time to remember."

"Oh, I've been putting my thinking cap on, I can tell you. . . . 'Course, I had him marked down long before he was done in."

"You did?"

"Son of cabinet minister. Foreign Office man. We were interested in the Foreign Office in those days. It wouldn't have made a first-rate story, but it would have been a nice little earner, if anyone had run it."

"Where did you do your researches? Who were your sources?"

"Well, for example, I'd hang around the clubs he went to." He leaned forward till he was closer than I liked, twisting his horrible old face into a lubricious grin. "Didn't go in, o' course: didn't want to feel strange hands around my hind quarters." (Looking at him now, and imagining what he looked like then, it struck me as eminently unlikely that he would have done.) "But I'd watch and see who did, and talk to some of the boys who came out with them afterwards. You had to be on the ball, so to speak, because these clubs sprang up overnight and vanished in the same way. Sometimes the police tolerated them for a bit and infiltrated, but sometimes they came down on them like a ton of bricks as soon as they twigged what they were. Over the years I built up a dossier, not just about young

Wycliffe, but about all sorts of people. Did you realize the Duke of —"

"Timothy Wycliffe!"

"Oh, all right. . . . Well, as I say, I got quite a lot of info on young Tim — where he went, where he picked 'em up, who his real pals were — his regular pals, as opposed to his one-night stands. I was just waiting for him to do something really outrageous, then all the editors I worked for would come running for the dirt on him. Trouble was, the outrageous thing he did was get murdered."

"What did you do then?"

"Well, of course I wanted to be the one who delivered the dirt on him and the nancy boy they said had murdered him. Naturally. Trouble was that in the days — weeks — after the murder, all the newspapers were full of was bloody Suez. By the time they got back to normal the story was as dead as a duck. The only thing that might have revived it was his murderer getting caught."

"Did you know anything about his murderer?"

"I had his name in my files. Andrew Forbes. Went around with Wycliffe, visited at his flat, all that sort of thing. I got that from his cleaner — Wycliffe's cleaner. As far as I was concerned he was a working-class lad who'd joined the hand-flapping brigade. Then, weeks, maybe months, after the murder I heard a whisper that he was working in a bar on Majorca. It was a pretty firm story. But in those days you didn't just hop on a plane and go. It cost money. I didn't need a photographer — I could do my own. In fact, I tell this mob" — he gave a derogatory handwave in the direction of the ten or twelve pairs of eyes that were still intent on us — "that I was the original of these Pappa-whatsits."

"Paparazzi."

"That's the ticket. You ever been followed by them, Mr. Proctor? Not interesting enough, I don't suppose. But anyway, it still cost money, and I needed a firm commitment from an editor that he'd run the story and play it big. But it was no go. All I got was shifts and evasions."

"Why do you think that was?"

"It was just after Suez, wasn't it? Tory party fortunes at rock bottom. They might have run the story when the party was riding high, but they weren't going to kick their party when it was down."

"But there were Labour papers."

"One or two. But they always got into a bit of a quandary when a story like that came up. The high moral tone didn't come natural to them. There were too many in the party who wanted to let the queers do what they liked provided they did it behind closed doors for them to be entirely easy when they were handed a story like I hoped to get hold of. . . . Makes you sick, doesn't it? . . . Mind you, it's not surprising. There was that Tom Driberg —"

"Yes, we all know about Tom Driberg."

"The things I had on him! Anyway, the long and the short of it was they wouldn't take it either. If it had been a cabinet minister I expect they'd have swallowed their scruples and sent me after it, but a cabinet minister's *son* . . . He just wasn't big enough, not worth the risk of alienating a lot of people in the party. So I never got to sunny Spain. . . . Mind you, I did wonder later on whether I hadn't been barking up the wrong tree."

"Why was that?"

"Well, it was a couple o' years later. They sent me up to Nottingham to dig up some dirt on this Alan Sillitoe — he was in the news, one of those Angry Young Men, and they wanted lots of dirt about what a hell-raiser he'd been, all the women he'd put in the club, just like the bloke in his book. . . . Dead loss it was: seems to have spent most of his time in the Public Library. . . . Anyway, it was nothing but dead ends, so I had plenty of time to spare, and I went along to this street where Andy Forbes used to live, and I talked to all the neighbours. Now, there were some that were shocked and there were some that were sorry, but there were none that I could find that had a hard word to say about Forbes when he was growing up in Nottingham, not one. . . . Got a fag?"

"I don't smoke."

Reluctantly he took out the packet I'd given him, opened it up, and lit one. The faces watching seemed to say "Basking in his moment of glory, isn't he?"

"Well, I thought that was odd. And eventually I knocked at his parents' home, and when his old man came to the door I put my foot in it and made sure I got all my questions answered. He was a nice enough bloke, upset of course, but I kept on at him, and what he said was that his boy had beaten up — well, what he said was 'had a fight with' — Timothy Wycliffe, because he'd been forced into bed with him. He'd beaten him up pretty badly, the father admitted that, but he'd definitely been alive when he left his flat. And thinking about it, that made sense to me."

"Why?"

"Well, quite a lot of my contacts at the time of the murder had insisted Forbes wasn't one of the limp-wristed brigade, and of course I'd said to myself, 'Like hell he wasn't.' And they'd said Tim and he weren't bed partners, and I'd said to myself 'Tell that to the marines.' Wasn't being cynical, just realistic. But all the neighbours and now the dad seemed to back this up. And I'd always worried about the phone being off the hook. I just couldn't see your nancy friend trying to telephone in the middle of the fight. It made more sense if he'd been left badly beaten up, had *then* tried to ring for help, and had then blacked out."

"Yes, I agree. But did you get any line on who might then have come along and finished him off?"

"No." He shook his head regretfully. "Could have been anyone, couldn't it? Any of his pals, for instance. Unbalanced, most of that lot. Get mad with jealousy. They're all either on a mad high or a mad low. Mind you, I didn't try very hard to find out. That was a story there was no hope of resurrecting."

"But you think someone just happened to come along, and took advantage of Tim's situation?"

"No, I don't. I think that would be too much of a coincidence. I think it was whoever he rang."

"But —"

"Because I'll tell you this: one thing a homosexual who'd been attacked by his boyfriend would not do in 1956 is ring the police. And I don't believe he'd ring ambulance either. I think he rang someone for help, and that was the help he got."

17

TWO NOBLE KINSMEN

On the road back to London, Sutcliffe and I discussed, and laughed about, the man we had just talked to.

"One of the things I remember about my really important cases," said Sutcliffe, a reminiscent expression on his face, "is that the men covering the case for Fleet Street, as it was then, always turned out to be so much more dislikeable than the criminal when we caught him. Terry is at the grubbier end of the spectrum for the sort of men I had to do with then."

"He is the pits," I agreed. "And don't his attitudes really take you back?"

"Maybe. I can see why you'd think that. But you've been cut off, all those years you've been minister. In fact you could hear the same in any East End pub today. Pardick has that dirty-minded relish that you always get at the lower end of the tabloid press. And that press knows its audience."

"I suppose so. Depressing thought. And yet, and yet . . ." I looked at him meaningfully to see if he agreed with me.

"What he said made sense," said Sutcliffe, nodding. "He was on to the innocence of Andy Forbes, which I take it is the assumption that we're working on. So far as we know no one else at the time had got there. And I'm damned sure he was right about not phoning the police. I don't like to say it, and I should have thought of it earlier, but we were the last people any homosexual in the fifties would put himself in the hands of voluntarily."

"Absolutely. The point about not ringing for an ambulance is more dubious, though, isn't it?"

"Not necessarily. The medical authorities could have felt duty-bound to inform the police about what had been a serious attack. He was also the sort of person who would have used private medicine anyway, isn't he?"

"I've no idea. Not necessarily. But in any case it may have been Tim's instinct in an emergency to get help from family or friends. Tim was always very hot on friendship."

We drove on in silence for some time, and then I said:

"I need to find a way to talk to Tim's brother."

We tossed this to and fro, wondering how

best to manage it, but Sutcliffe's experience was mainly of turning up on a doorstep, flashing his ID, and then asking questions. Clearly something else was needed here, but I was hampered by knowing nothing about Tim's brother beyond the fact — gleaned from Marjorie's way of speaking about him — that he is still alive. When I got back home I tried to ring Marjorie, intending a bit of tactically vague questioning, but there was no reply. I sat thinking for a bit, and then got to work with *Burke's Peerage* and *Who's Who*. I came up with the information that the address for both Lord John Wycliffe and James Wycliffe was Maddern Hall, near Formby, in the county of Avon. Now that I did find interesting.

Tonight over dinner I talked it over with Jeremy. He was in favour of my using my old ministerial clout to barge straight in on them and ask my questions. I think he would rather have liked to come along to this bearding of father and son. He is getting quite involved in the matter, though in a much more light-hearted way. I told him I felt that would be counterproductive. Jeremy thought there would have to be some sort of trick to get the son out of the way so that I could talk to Lord John. I had to agree that getting to talk to Tim's father alone might well present a problem, but I pointed out that even if James were got out of the way, there was presumably still the wife, who I had gathered was the more formidable of the pair. Ways of getting both out of the way and leaving me in the house did not present themselves readily.

"Who is James Wycliffe anyway?" asked Jeremy. "I mean *what* is he? What is his claim to fame?"

"He has been Lord Lieutenant of Avon," I answered. "Otherwise he is described as 'farmer.' "

"You don't think my ringing at a prearranged time and saying 'T'owd cow'ave got into clover meadow' would do the trick, do you?" asked Jeremy, his mock-rural accent gloriously bad.

"No, I don't. I think he must have scraped into *Who's Who* by a combination of his birth, his Lord Lieutenancy, and his being a very big farmer indeed. So I don't see him being the sort who drags on his wellies and stumps out after stray cows, let alone one who takes his lady wife along with him. But thanks for the thought. As for the accent, don't ring us . . ."

So tonight I am left pondering, without any firm plan, but with the strongest possible desire to get to see Tim's other surviving relatives.

* * *

Three days after I wrote the above, yesterday, I went down to Formby. I drove down with little more than the shadow of a notion of what I would do when I got there. I went, reluctantly, on my own. I loathe motorway driving on a weekday — loathed it, in fact, even when I had a chauffeur doing it for me in a ministerial limousine — so there was no chance of thinking as I went. Nor did the much narrower roads after I'd left the motorway encourage anything but dedicated concentration. At a few minutes after eleven I stopped at a gap in the grass verge where there was a gate into a meadow and surveyed the ordinance survey map I'd provided myself with.

Formby is just two miles within Avon, near the boundary with Gloucestershire. Of course twenty years ago it would have been *in* Gloucestershire. When I was in the government I couldn't say it, but now I can: I abhor and detest the reorganisation of the British counties undertaken by the first administration of which I was a member. What a botched, misconceived, antihistorical job it was! Why, in fact, do it at all? Does anybody today say "I am an Avon man" with the pride he might say "I am a Yorkshireman" or "I am a Cornishman"? Of course not! I doubt even a young man, one who never knew the old counties, would say it. We have destroyed the pride of centuries for supposed administrative advantages which never materialised. Sermon over. So anyway here I was in Avon, of which James Wycliffe had been Lord Lieutenant. I calculated I was three miles from Formby, and a mere one and a half from Maddern Hall.

I set off for the Hall, driving slowly. The road was narrow, and of the rolling-English-drunkard variety. I passed through a hamlet called Nethley: a post-office-cum-shop and about eight small houses, one of them for sale. A quarter of a mile down the road, on my left, I found the gates to Maddern Hall — open, giving a view of a handsome early nineteenth-century manor house: not a large one, but a regular and satisfying one. It had a Jane Austeny feel to it which I relished — red brick, warm, inviting. The drive up was lined by trees, and around and behind it rolled acres and acres of excellent farming land.

And ahead of me along the road were three cottages, no doubt once tied to one or other of the various farms in the area. I drove on slowly, and saw that the one nearest the gates had a For Sale sign up. Now that could be a stroke of luck! The agents were named as Wetherfield and Markham, of Formby. I drove on and took the first turning that would take me there.

Formby was little more than a large village. The girl in the outer office of Wetherfield and Markham's looked at me without recognition, and without a great deal of interest either. She nodded routinely when I named the cottage I was interested in, and rummaged in a drawer for the key.

"There's still furniture in the property," she said in a rote-learned voice. "Mr. Wycliffe will arrange a house clearance, unless the buyer wants to come to some other arrangement."

"I see. Is that Mr. James Wycliffe of Maddern Hall?"

"That's right."

"Ah. I once knew his brother."

She looked quite blank, as well she might, being hardly over twenty. Even in the country scandals do eventually die.

"Any questions or offers should come through us," she intoned, in the sort of voice better suited to making "tuppence off" announcements in supermarkets.

"Of course. I wouldn't dream of troubling Mr. Wycliffe," I lied.

I told her I would have lunch before I went to view the cottage, and asked where I might go. She said, "There's the Plough," rather in the manner of someone behind the counter of a Soviet food store reciting the one sort of sausage they had in stock. So the Plough it was, and it seemed warm and comfortable enough, with a real fire going and a few early-lunchtime drinkers. It would probably have been safer to order a sandwich, but to get on the landlord's good side I ordered steak and kidney pie (with chips, naturally), and a pint of his best bitter.

"I'm on my way to look over a cottage out near Nethley."

"Oh aye? Would that be old Mr. Dereham's as was?"

"I'm not sure. Belongs to Mr. James Wycliffe, I gather."

"That'll be it. It's all Mr. James's now, or it is in effect. . . . Very nice gentleman, is Mr. James."

There seemed to be an "as opposed to" implied here, so I crinkled up my forehead as if in thought and said: "I have a feeling my late wife knew his wife."

"Ah!" said the landlord, and tapped his nose. "Different kettle of fish entirely, is Mrs. James. More than a touch of the tartar. A fair woman, mind you, but likes her own way. You take my advice: if you buy the cottage, you keep on the right side of her! . . . Haven't I seen you before somewhere?"

"Not round here. You could have seen me on the television."

"Ah, that'd be it. It's always on in the back of the bar. I only see it with half an eye."

"That's much the best way to see it."

He showed a rare and commendable lack of curiosity about what I did when I appeared on the box. I could have been a glove-puppeteer for all he cared. I took my plate of steak and kidney and chips to a table in a corner, and read a paper while I forked it in. It was about what one would expect in a pub which had no competition in the provision of lunches in its village. I got the landlord to put an extra half-pint in my glass, but he was too busy to talk. Then I was ready to drive back to Maddern Hall.

I parked outside the cottage and made the ritual tour of inspection. It was conservatively furnished, a little dark, as cottages always are, but well-equipped and — until recently, I guessed — lovingly cared for. The garden, too, had been weeded and tidied not so long before. I wondered idly whether a country cottage might not be a good idea: I could write here, come for weekends, potter around in the garden. I wondered whether Jeremy would come. Probably, but I'd always be thinking he'd prefer to be in London, with friends of his own age. The inspection over, I locked the place up, reversed the car up the road, then turned into the gates of Maddern Hall and drove up the handsome, tree-lined approach to the house. Childe Roland to the Dark Tower came — though the only ghost that might be watching my approach was the ghost of Timothy Wycliffe.

I paused for a moment as I got out of the car and surveyed the well-kept lawns, the few but meticulously weeded flower beds, and the lush acreage stretching into the distance, dotted with farms, and with barns, hen runs, and piggeries. Then I walked up to the entrance and rang the bell.

"Yes?"

It was a daily woman who opened the door — aproned, with a duster in her hand.

"My name is Proctor, and I was wondering if Mr. or Mrs. —"

"What is it, Mary?"

The voice was well-bred, confident, unimaginative. I looked past the daily woman at the figure who now came into the oak-lined entrance hall. Unmistakably this was Mrs. Wycliffe. She was tall, with an indisputable air of command. There was no ostentation about her: she was simply dressed in a jumper and skirt of the kind that Ann often sported, and she wore no jewellery — swine before pearls had presumably been the

Wycliffe business motto. She had square shoulders and an erect stance, and she was without question a woman who expected and exacted deference.

"Mrs. Wycliffe?" I said, smiling deferentially (I had had much practice). "I don't think we've met but I'm —"

"Proctor. Peter Proctor. Well, this is a surprise. And an honour, of course. Do come in."

As I stepped over the threshold I breathed a sigh of relief. Marjorie Knopfmeyer had not passed on my interest in Timothy Wycliffe. Otherwise this woman, I felt sure, would be neither surprised nor welcoming. First hurdle over.

"I've just been looking at your cottage that's for sale," I explained. "The girl at Wetherfield and Markham's told me it was yours, and I thought I should come over and pay my respects. Lord John — as he then was — was a minister when I first entered the Commons."

"Well, I'm *most* pleased you're interested in the cottage, and so will James be." The tone was distinctly warm, even genial. "Do come through. Holiday home?"

"That's right. Not just that, though: place for getting down to my memoirs."

"James. Surprise guest. Peter Proctor."

She had ushered me into a long, airy living room, pleasantly furnished with family pieces

277

and rather dull pictures. James Wycliffe got up from the sofa, shook my hand with an expression of surprise, and we went through the ritual of greetings and explanations. He was a heavy, slightly florid man, with the kindly air of a person who knows he is not a great brain. He gave the impression of being someone who had never been his own master, and didn't much regret it. He had a dog at his feet, and he looked the type who would always have a dog somewhere in the vicinity.

"We were just going to have coffee," said Mrs. Wycliffe. "I'm Caroline, by the way. You'll have some with us, won't you? Excuse me — I won't be too long. We don't have any staff to speak of any longer."

"Well!" said James Wycliffe, settling down again into his sofa. "This is a pleasant variation to the day's routine. Damned pleased you're interested in the cottage. Even if you're not, it was civil of you to drop in. Mind you, we don't have all that much to do with politics these days."

"Me neither. I'm a dead letter, like your father. I was telling your wife that he was a minister when I first went into the Commons. I know your sister slightly, by the way — charming woman. And I was great friends with your brother."

His face fell at once, in what seemed utterly

genuine regret. My first impression was that he was a man innocent of guile.

"Tim. Poor old Tim. I've never stopped grieving for him. Now there was a man with gifts. There was a man who could win people to him. I'm a plain sort of chap, but even I could see that. What a waste! How did you know him?"

"At the Foreign Office. He and I started more or less together. We were very different types — like you I'm a plain sort of chap. I got where I did get through a thoroughly boring competence. But I couldn't fail to see his distinction, and be influenced by him."

"Didn't know you'd started in the F.O."

"Just for a few years. I got out and went into industry. Couldn't stand Eden's way with his staff. Tim was thinking of getting out before he died, wasn't he?"

"Oh yes. Not for that reason, I don't think. He realized he was a fish out of water there. He used to say he'd gone in because he was interested in foreign countries, and he'd found that the F.O. was the last place that anyone with that interest ought to go. Damned witty chap, Tim. My father and I both told him it would be disloyal to get out during Suez, and I'm glad to say we convinced him. But the F.O. was never the place for him: he wasn't discreet or hypocritical enough for the high-ups there."

"I felt that at the time. I was always warning him that he was much too . . . open. He was thinking of going to work for the Hatherley Trust, wasn't he?"

"That's right. He was to be their spokesman. Damned good job he'd have made of it too. Better than the chap who *did* run it who was always on television at one time, whatever his name was. . . . Of course one can say that now. . . ."

"Not at the time?"

"Definitely not at the time! A hot potato if ever I knew one, especially if Father was around. And I've got to admit we both tried to step on it firmly at the time. But times have changed, haven't they? Attitudes have changed."

"I think they have, to some extent. But you say you were against his working for them when the matter came up?"

He shook his head in self-depreciation.

"Wasn't a question of what I was against. Tim and I were great friends, but he'd never have come to me for advice. Quite right too. I'm a frightful old stick-in-the-mud, always have been. It was a question of what Father said."

"No, I suppose Lord John wouldn't have been too happy."

"Putting it mildly. We were staying with him in the Kensington house at the time. We had a house in Formby then, and acted as unofficial liaison with the constituency people. All the time the crisis was on we were back and forth, back and forth. Father and Caroline were always very close politically — she was secretary, nursemaid and cheerleader to him, all unpaid. She'd have made a damned good MP if things had been different in the party then. Anyway, I remember we were just congratulating ourselves on having persuaded Tim he shouldn't resign till after it was all over when he dropped into a phone call to me just what he intended to do when he did resign. I'm not too bright, but I felt a bit uneasy about it. When I told Father he hit the roof."

"What happened?"

"Well, the trouble was Tim didn't think Father was the person to give him advice either."

"I'm not altogether surprised. He seldom talked about him. They weren't close, were they?"

"No. Tim was quite right. He was a free spirit, and he had to make his own decisions. But you couldn't expect Father to see it like that. There was a blistering telephone conversation the night before he died. The atmosphere in the house was positively crackling.

Caroline and I were in the sitting room and I tell you: we shivered! We couldn't hear what was said, but we could hear Father shouting. He could be tremendous at moments like that . . . Terrifying . . . But of course in the long run it wouldn't have done any good. Tim would have gone his own way."

"Who would have gone his own way?"

Caroline Wycliffe had come in with a coffee pot and cups on a tray, and began setting out cups before us and pouring.

"Tim would, dear. We were talking about Tim."

There was an immediate frosting in the atmosphere.

"What an unfortunate topic of conversation when we have the good fortune to have a cabinet minister visit us!"

"Ex," I said. "I knew your brother-in-law well, Mrs. Wycliffe."

"As far as I'm concerned the least said about Tim the better," she said, her mouth in a hard, straight line.

"Dammit, Caroline, I loved Tim!" protested her husband. "I'm not going to have him talked about as if he should be swept away under the carpet!"

"I was fond of Tim myself," said Caroline coldly, "at least when he wasn't being outrageous. I'd be the first to admit that he was wonderfully clever at talking me around. But in view of some of his activities I don't think he is a suitable topic for social chitchat."

"For God's sake, Caroline! Your father was an admiral! Do you think that sort of thing isn't a matter of everyday occurrence in the navy?"

She shook her head, as if in acknowledgement that this was one subject on which she could not bully her husband round to her opinion. She took up a cup and got up from the sofa.

"I'll take this in to Father."

"Still pretty bright?"

"Not too bad."

"He's having one of his good days," said James in explanation. "Generally speaking he's declining fast into senility."

"Really? I saw him not long ago in the House of Lords."

"Ah well — senility no bar there, eh?" James laughed heartily, then thought he'd been unfeeling. "But that will be the last time, I'm afraid. Dereham, whose cottage you looked at, used to take him. Father's old butler, with him for years. Only five years younger, as a matter of fact, but much spryer. They let him look after Father right up to the entrance of the Chamber. I think a lot of people thought he *was* a peer. He had a stroke three weeks ago. Sad. I don't think Father's taken it in yet."

I had listened to Mrs. Wycliffe's footsteps and they had not gone upstairs. I said: "He looked very frail."

"That's right. He has one of the drawing rooms down here as his room — he eats and sleeps there nowadays. It's a big burden on Caroline, though we get help now and then. Mind you, in some ways it's a relief."

"Oh?"

"He's not looking over our shoulders the whole time. When he lost his seat in 1966 it was the end of the world for him: he was absolutely adrift, poor old man. He put all his energies into the running of this place: acquired more farms, spread himself, reformed work practices. Trouble was, he wasn't really very good at running a large farming business."

"Penny-pinching," said Caroline, coming back and taking up her coffee. "Sorry to say it about the old man, but that's the size of it. Penny-pinching just doesn't do in farming, and it puts the local people's backs up."

"But Father never was awfully good with *people*, was he, Caro? He got his life Peerage in 1973. Lord Edmonton. Nobody thinks of him as that, though, and he often even forgets it himself. Still, it gave him a toehold on political life again. About that time he made over Maddern and all the estate to us, to avoid death duties. Always resented taxes, poor old Father. So we ran the place, but we always had him looking over our shoulders. Meanwhile he stayed on here, practically alone with Dereham, who lived in the cottage and was pretty much the last of the staff. Funny situation: they spent all day here together, quarrelling and getting on each other's nerves, but somehow needing each other."

"Rather like one of these modern plays," said Caroline surprisingly.

"We always encouraged him to be active in the Lords — to get him out of our hair. Caroline is a marvellous administrator, and I — well, I suppose I supply the human touch. Amiable old buffer. Anyway eventually we had to move in. Dereham couldn't look after him on his own any more, let alone the place, which was going to rack and ruin. So we've been with him for some years now, but we've always felt him looking disapprovingly at practically everything we've done. At least until recently."

"You have a son to take over?"

"Grandson. Son was in on computers at an early stage. Has Caro's brain, luckily. No interest in the place at all. But Ben, fortunately, has loved it from the moment he opened his eyes and started taking notice. He's here now, learning about the place from the fieldwork upwards. Lovely to have him here."

"I've never understood," said Caroline, "how it helps to learn the business of running a large estate to go out into the fields and hoe turnips. A course in accountancy would be more use, but I suppose he'll do that eventually. Ah well, I'm old-fashioned, thank goodness. If that's what Ben wants, let him do it. He's a help with Father, too."

"I'd like to pay my respects to Lord John — Lord Edmonton — before I go," I said.

"I don't think so," said Caroline quickly. Then she flushed at her rudeness. "I'm sorry, but I always feel it's not kind to old people . . . it makes an exhibition of them . . . I mean when they're a shadow of their former selves."

"Nonsense, Caroline. You know Father is tickled pink by anything connected with politics. He'll be immensely flattered that he's still remembered."

"No, I don't think it would be a good idea at all." Her head swung around. "What on earth is that?"

Her eye had been caught by something through the window. She got up and James and I rose from our seats with her. Parked just behind my own Volvo was a rather dirty old van with "D. O'CONNOR, MILKMAN" on the side. In the back was a large shape covered with a tarpaulin, and getting out of the driver's seat was Marjorie Knopfmeyer. I recognised her with a lift of the heart: could she be my way out of a ticklish situation? We were all in the entrance hall when she rang the doorbell and marched straight in.

"Caroline! James! I've got the most marvellous present for you, which you're going to *hate* — oh, Good Lord — Peter!"

She was surprised, but the next moment she shot me a dazzling smile that was instinct with intelligent apprehension of the cause of my being there.

"Oh, you know Mr. Proctor, Marjorie?" James burbled on. "Oh yes, he said you'd met. He's just dropped in . . ."

"Of course I know Peter. Good friends. Now the thing is this: I'm back at the cottage now, as you know, but I find I've been left this marvellous piece by Ferdy — *The Fall of Icarus*. One of his really fine works. He sold it to a very rich lady, one of our Gloucester neighbours, and since she had no near relatives she left it back to me in her will. Wonderful windfall, but I've nowhere to put it at the cottage — *far* too large. So I thought: that's just the thing for the lawns in front of Maddern. It's meant for outside, of course.

So I got the milkman to lend me his van and here it is. You'll loathe it, Caroline, but it's rather valuable and generally considered one of Ferdy's masterpieces. You'll have sculpture buffs peering at it through the gates. Come on, come and have a look. Could you get Ben to help me unload it?"

She took her sister-in-law firmly by the arm. Caroline said: "How interesting. We'll all go and have a look." She shot a glance at her husband which I had no difficulty interpreting, but she let herself be led away. In the hall James fussed for a moment and then said:

"Like to have a little talk to Father? Old chap would be pleased as Punch. Loves anything to do with politics. I'll make it right with Caroline."

I thanked him and he led me to a dark door under an archway in a covered nook at the rear of the hall. When he opened it he took me into a room flooded with light, with windows giving on to lawns and fields, yet somehow I could not rid myself of the notion that I was being led into the dark tower's darkest inner sanctum.

18

DARK CENTRE

James Wycliffe led me over to a high-backed chair placed near a blazing fire, with the figure in it hidden from me. I could feel the son's nervousness from his hand on my arm. The room was light and airy, with windows on two sides giving a glorious view of lawns, hedges, and fields beyond. As I approached the chair I seemed to see only rugs, but there in the middle was the shrunken figure I had seen at the House of Lords — a wizened, depleted body, with sunken cheeks and downcast eyes, something once a man, but now, it seemed, diminishing out of life.

"Father, you have a visitor," said James, in that hearty tone so many children eventually adopt to their ageing parents. "It's Peter Proctor who used to be minister of . . . of —"

"Energy, among other things," I said. I hope I felt suitably humbled that a life-long Conservative could not remember what I had been or what I had done. I was further chastened by the first words that emerged from the chair.

"Dreadful crew. No style. No style at all."

There was malice in the voice, vitriol even, that was unaccountable and frightening.

"Yes," I said meekly. "I suppose we do lack style."

"Still a minister, are you?"

"Not any longer."

"Rats leaving a sinking ship."

"Thrown off actually," I said. Then I added, trying not to be cowed: "Though I've often wondered what a sensible rat on a sinking ship is supposed to do if not leave."

"I was thrown off a sinking ship. . . ." The voice was now brooding, thick with grievance, and it seemed to reach me through aeons of time, heavy with rancour and vindictiveness. I was conscious of James Wycliffe tiptoeing out of the room, no doubt making his escape from an encounter that was not bearing out his notion that his father would be "tickled pink" by a visitor from the world of politics. The voice droned on.

"That bounder Macmillan . . . ungrateful swine. . . . He'd have done anything to save his own skin. . . . Still, he had style. Eden had style. Churchill had style."

"I served under Selwyn Lloyd," I said to

redress the balance. It was the wrong thing to say. I was astonished by the furious hiss from the chair.

"I should have had that job! I should have been Foreign Secretary! It's what I'd prepared myself for all my life! I was kept down in piddling jobs — Minister of Planning, Minister for Local Government. Beneath me! . . ." The fury in the voice was chilling. But then he seemed altogether to cast a chill on the warm, sunny room. The head withdrew itself within the blankets for a moment. The voice was more normal when he said: "You were in the Foreign Office?"

"Yes, under Morrison and Eden, then under Lloyd."

"Lloyd! I should have gone there!"

"I worked with your son Timothy."

"Rotten apple . . . no loyalty . . ." I was suddenly conscious of dark, venomous eyes turned towards me, transfixing me. "You the chap that's been going round asking questions?"

This really pulled me up sharp. I had no answer prepared.

"Yes."

"Damned interference. No business of yours."

"He was my friend."

"I know all about Tim's friends."

"Friend, not lover. . . . How did you know

about my questions? Your children don't."

"Dereham picked it up when we were at the House of Lords. Told me about it on the way home. Chuckled. He knew a thing or two that he shouldn't have known. . . . Dereham's dead. They think I haven't taken it in, but I have. I know he's dead . . . be dead myself before the year's out. Then you can write what you like. Until then you'd better be damned careful!"

He seemed to have shrunk further into the rugs, and it was as if the vicious tones were issuing from a dark hole. I tried to talk normally to the hole, as if I were interviewing the old man on the telephone.

"You had a row with Timothy just before he was killed, didn't you?"

"James and Caroline been talking?" He pulled himself round painfully and looked at me. For the first time I saw full-face and felt the vicious power of his eyes. I seemed to be shrivelled by a rage and a resentment that had been preserved intact over the decades. "They said nothing to the police. They're mediocrities, but loyal ones. Caroline has all her wits about her."

"You had a row about the job Tim was going to take, didn't you?"

"Yes."

"You thought it would be . . . bad publicity for you?"

"Should have thought that was damned obvious. Every time he made a statement to the press, spoke on the wireless or television — if they'd let him on there, which I doubt, because they had different standards then — it would have been 'said Mr. Timothy Wycliffe, son of the present Minister of Planning,' 'son of the Local Government Minister.' . . . It would have been ruinous. He should never have thought of it. The boy had no sense of loyalty."

"It was something Tim felt strongly about, something he thought was very important."

"More important than my career? That says something about his judgement, doesn't it? I didn't notice the laws had much effect on the way he lived his life. Or most of his friends either. But he was willing to jeopardise everything because of his piffling little campaign for queers."

"Jeopardise your career, you mean."

"That's what I said. He was my son. It should have been important to him."

I felt a wave of depression, as if my dim political career and his dim political career had somehow coalesced. On the lawns outside a little group of people had come into view. The old man's children had been joined by his great-grandson, a stocky, genial boy in dirty Wellington boots and a heavy khaki pull-over. He looked normal and well-disposed, and I marvelled at how little of this man's consuming malevolence seemed to have passed down to his descendents. The boy and James had been carrying with difficulty a massive object covered by a tarpaulin, and now, supervised by Marjorie, they set it up on its base. Caroline said something to James and glanced towards the house, but he shook his head, pulled at her sleeve and directed her attention back to the statue. They all began to pull at the tarpaulin.

"You can do nothing about it, you know."

The voice came with whiplash scorn from the pathetic bundle of humanity in the chair. The rugs, the voice, the venom — I was suddenly reminded of Grandfather Smallweed and was tempted to give him a good shake-up to prevent his disappearing entirely into the rugs. I needed some sign of my physical superiority to counteract the scorn, the poison, and above all what lay behind them — a note of triumph, as if he were scoring one last victory — a victory over me.

"You can do nothing at all. I'm ninety . . . ninety-something, failing a bit in my mind — though nowhere near as much as *they* think. . . . No one would do anything at all."

"I know."

"Soon I'll be meeting the maker I've never

believed in. . . . I've been a regular churchgoer all my life until recently, but I've never had any time for that stuff. . . . Such nonsense! Like a child clutching on to any old hand for security. . . . We come from nothing and we go to nothing. . . . I don't give a damn for your questions. There's nothing you can do. I'm not afraid and I'm not ashamed."

"Tell me how the quarrel ended, then."

"It ended with his threatening me. That's what that fine young man whom everybody loved did: threatened his own father."

"Oh?" This was new, but it tied up with something I'd thought about before: it had never seemed to me that Tim's job with the Hatherley Trust was enough. I asked eagerly: "What did he threaten you with?"

"I'm not going to tell you." He turned painfully again to look me straight in the face, and there was an unpleasant smile of derision on his face, as if he were teasing me: teasing me because I could do nothing with his confession, but teasing me too because there was something that I would never know, however much I might probe. He reminded me of a school bully — not the sort who enjoyed beating or beating up his juniors, but the sort who tormented them in much more subtle ways. He tormented me by dangling further information in front of me. "It was something he overheard one day, when he was a young boy. It was his birthday. He and his mother were waiting outside my study — Tim was to get my present to him. That was the way we did it with all the children. They didn't knock because they heard me on the phone. So they just stood there waiting, and they heard what I was saying on the phone."

"And that was what Tim threatened you with?"

"Yes. Damnable treachery."

"And you and he had never talked about it till the day before he died?"

"Never." The vicious eye glinted in the firelight. "Evelyn and I did, once or twice. She was a pathetic, conventional creature. I think she went and wept on Dereham's shoulder too. There's no other way he could have known. What fools women are! A butler! But Tim never let on when he came in for his present, nor for a while after. But I gradually realised I didn't have his respect. Imagine it: a boy of twelve looking at his father and judging him! As if he could understand. I came to hate that look. . . ."

"But he never brought it out into the open?"

"Never, until all those years later."

"And you decided to kill him?"

"Of course I didn't, you fool!" The voice held immeasurable scorn. He was a man who had a deep need to feel scorn. "But I *wanted* to kill him."

"No, that's right. You didn't *decide* to kill him until you got his phone call, did you?"

"Of course not."

"The phone call intended for Marjorie."

"That's right. They loved each other, those two. Nobody ever realised — but then they thought his nancy boy had killed him — that his first instinct would be to call Marjorie, or failing her James. She was out at some damned demonstration, and James and Caroline had gone down to Gloucestershire to test feeling in the constituency." He paused. "So he got me."

There was, horribly, relish in his tone.

"And it was perfect, wasn't it, in circumstances and time?"

"Perfect."

"I used to get the Suez angle wrong," I said, keeping my voice normal, free of anger. "I used to think the coincidence that it happened during Suez was the reason I and everybody else remembered so little about it. That was to get it the wrong way round. The fact is that it was only during Suez that it could have happened at all — you could almost say it happened because of Suez."

He nodded with a smile that was almost complacent. I went on:

"Because only during Suez could it be done practically without publicity. Any other time and the popular newspapers would have blazoned it on the front pages: 'Minister's son killed by male lover.' 'Another homosexual scandal in the Foreign Office.' As it was it became a tiny item tucked away on an inside page."

"He was a fool!" The old man rasped it out. How he loved calling people fools! "He should have said nothing when he heard me answer. He knew he had threatened me the day before. Forfeited the right to consider himself my son. Instead of which he said: 'I'm hurt. I need help.' My heart leapt up in me. I said: 'What's happened? Who's hurt you?' And he said: 'A friend.' Then he blacked out. A friend! Pathetic little pervert! I knew at once what had happened. He had made up my mind for me."

Outside on the lawn they had got the tarpaulin off the statue. A human figure, seemingly a child of the air, but hurtling through it to his destruction. From his arms hung tattered fragments of wings, remnants of his aspirations and hopes. It was a figure of dazzling vitality, of movement, and of terror. From the way the little group stood around it I had the impression that they all, even Caroline, were impressed.

"It was nearly half past nine," said the voice from the chair, still with that teasing quality underlying its bitterness. "I'd been about to leave, to vote in the division at ten. Three-line whip, Labour censure motion. I could do what I'd decided to do and still get to Westminster for the vote. I took the key Marjorie had for the flat — I knew where it hung in the kitchen. I drove from Kensington to Belgravia in five minutes and left the car in the Square. But I took the jack from the boot. It was the only heavy thing I could think of on the spur of the moment. I slipped into the mews, went up the stairs and opened the door. . . ."

He stopped — for breath, not for pity.

"Was Tim still passed out?"

"No. He was lying there on the floor, sobbing. I've never in my life seen anything so unmanly. A grown man crying because he'd had a fight with his boyfriend. An out-of-work electrician! To think I'd spawned *that.* . . . I'd put the jack down on the landing outside. I took it up, brought it down in one blow on his head, then I made sure he was dead and took the jack back to the car. I made the division lobby and voted. On the way home I threw the jack in the Thames. It was all perfectly simple."

"Simple," I said. "You make it all sound

a matter of course."

"It was."

"If Andrew Forbes had been charged, would you have confessed?"

The sunken face smiled scornfully.

"Don't be childish."

"You felt no remorse at all?"

"None whatsoever." He was both challenging me and telling the truth. Challenging my bourgeois code, yet being truthful about his lack of one. He felt superior to others not only in what he thought of as his greater intelligence, but also in his lack of moral scruples. He was a superior being, a man who could — who did — stand outside conventional codes. "The boy, as I said, was a rotten apple. He had to be thrown out of the barrel. And he'd threatened me — his own father!" He paused. The eyes glinted again in the firelight, pinpoints of malicious light. "And you'll never know what he threatened me with!"

Something stirred in me — some memory, a collection of memories. As I stood there watching him in his empty triumph they jumped and danced together in my mind, and they made a pattern.

"I don't believe Tim threatened you. Threatening wasn't Tim's style at all."

"He did, as good as."

"I think you accused him of disloyalty — you've used the word over and over today. And I think Tim said something like: 'Disloyalty — that's a thing you know all about.' "

There came over his face an expression not of fear, but of petulance, as if I had spoilt his game. He feared he was going to be baulked of his triumph. He said nothing.

"Tim would have been twelve in 1939."

I had seen Tim's birthdate in the *Peerage,* but I'd forgotten it. But I remember Tim saying, "I'm a Virgo, believe it or not."

"Was he twelve, perhaps, on or around the third of September 1939?"

Still he said nothing, though he pouted. I heard in my ears Harry Wratton's voice: "Tim said the most apparently respectable and upright people were Fifth Columnists."

"So Tim and your wife were waiting outside your study door, and they heard you talking to — who was it? All the way to Ribbentrop in Berlin? Or the German ambassador in London? And you were assuring him, were you not, that the declaration of war was a great mistake, that you'd be doing all in your power to get the two nations together again, that you'd be putting Germany's point of view quietly to the people running the country, that the person Europe should be fighting was Stalin — all the stuff people like you had been saying for years. Only you went on saying it. That was it, wasn't it?"

"It was the only policy that made sense. You wouldn't expect a boy of twelve to understand that!"

"I don't think the man of twenty-seven understood it either. He regarded you as tantamount to a traitor."

"I told you: the boy was a fool."

"Then I'm glad to think of myself as a fool alongside him. And it was for fear of his talking that you killed him, wasn't it?"

He fixed me with his bright, terrible eyes. His voice came with a mad intensity.

"It would have been the end to me, the end of my political career."

I remembered that Lord John Wycliffe had been dismissed, along with six other cabinet ministers, in Harold Macmillan's Night of the Long Knives in 1962.

I shivered. Then I turned on my heels and left the room.

Out on the lawns they were still admiring *The Fall of Icarus.* As I approached I caught a glance from Caroline Wycliffe that was shot through with fear and uncertainty. It told me that she, at least, had some suspicions of what had happened that November night in 1956. I kept my face blank of all expression. I was introduced to her grandson Ben — a frank, endearing boy with a cherubic face, not unlike my son Christopher's. I stood looking at the statue — the vital, plummetting body with its singed wings. There was in it a wonderful sense of energy, but also one of waste. Marjorie looked at me, and I nodded slightly.

"Father was all right?" asked Caroline, a tremor in her voice.

"Perfectly all right. Quite *au fait* with things. We had a good talk about politics in the fifties."

It was not until yesterday might, after I got back from Avon, that I could bring Jeremy up to date.

"And there was no shame when he talked about it?" he asked.

"None whatsoever. If anything, satisfaction."

"You'll write that book, won't you?"

"Yes, I think I will. The man will be dead before the year's out, and he knows it."

"I think you should. But the Wycliffes will fight you every inch of the way."

"I'm sure they will. The James Wycliffes anyway. But Caroline Wycliffe has suspected and kept quiet about it. I don't have a great deal of sympathy with her."

"It will set the record straight."

"I think I owe it to Tim. And to Andy Forbes."

"It will be a lot more interesting to write than the memoirs."

"Infinitely more. To write and to read. And there doesn't seem any more useful work in the offing. No whiff of a peerage. No more mention of that place on the Royal Commission. It seems I'm still not forgiven at Number Ten."

Jeremy looked up at me smiling.

"It's not that, you know. Surely you must have realised? You're not considered a good risk any longer. They've found out about us, Dad."

I wish he wouldn't call me Dad. It underlines the gap in our ages. My children all call me Pop.

"I expect you're right," I said.

I put my arm around him and we went up to bed.